# LARGE PRINT

# RACING THE HUNTER'S MOON

UNDER THE HOOD SERIES, BOOK 3

SALLY CLEMENTS

Copyright © 2020 by Sally Clements

All rights reserved.

No part of this book may be reproduced in any form or by any electronic or mechanical means, including information storage and retrieval systems, without written permission from the author, except for the use of brief quotations in a book review.

## ABOUT THE BOOK...

This story, Racing the Hunter's Moon, is the third book in the Under the Hood series, and is Betty's story.

# ONE

"Excuse me."

At the deep voice behind her, Betty Smith swung around, practically colliding with a wide expanse of navy-blue T-shirt stretched over an impressive chest. Her gaze tracked upward, over muscles skimmed by light cotton, to a strong column of neck and a superhero jawline, barely covered by a hint of five o'clock shadow. Was it soft to the touch or would it tickle against her cheek? Looking higher, her gaze collided with midnight-blue eyes staring into hers with an intensity that stole the air from her lungs.

He was crazy hot. The straight nose, pronounced cheekbones, and those eyes might in another face have combined to handsome, but the intense physicality of the stranger and the way his eyes blazed through her made him devastating.

"Yes?" The odds of coming face-to-face with a gorgeous stranger on Meadowsweet's Main Street were pretty low. She thought she knew everyone in this town, but she'd certainly never seen him before. If only she didn't have something else to do… She glanced up the alley. Her quarry was escaping.

"Don't even think about it." The stranger's black eyebrows pulled together in a scowl.

The romantic daydream dissolved instantly. Betty took a step back. "Don't even think about what?" Every minute she stood here, Charmers was getting away. A chance sighting of him from the window of the bakery had made her abandon her aim of buying pastries and hurry out to follow him. He'd been walking down Main Street, and moments ago had ducked into the alley between the bank and the dry cleaner's. She had to know where he was going—if he was meeting anyone.

"You're about to blow it." The stranger's mouth tightened.

Betty brought her hands up, palm out.

"Listen, I don't know what you're talking about, but…"

"If you follow Charmers down there"—he gestured in the direction of the alley—"you're playing right into his hands. There is nothing down there, no store entrances. The alley is a dead end. You've been creeping along after him for ten minutes, and I reckon he wants to confirm his suspicion that you're following him. He's going to turn around and walk back, and if he finds you following him, the game is up."

Adrenaline raced through Betty's veins. *Who is this guy? And how does he know I'm following Charmers?* Her fingers curled into fists. The con man who cheated her mother had been working alone—at least she'd always presumed he'd been working alone. What if she was wrong; what if this was his accomplice?

"Look, I'm not the bad guy here. Just walk away." The stranger jerked his head back in the direction she'd come from.

"I will not." Betty squared her shoulders.

The stranger glanced up the alley. "Shit." He grabbed her arm and tried to tug her away, huffing out a frustrated breath when she refused to move. "He's coming back, goddammit."

Before she had a chance to react, he forced her up against the dry cleaner's window and pressed his mouth onto hers. Eyes wide, she tried to jerk her head back, but couldn't, as the wall was behind her.

His mouth was closed, and his eyes stared into hers, flashing anger. He'd positioned himself to hide her from view, with one arm around her as if they were a loving couple, while his other grasped her upper arm.

Betty pushed both hands against his chest, but he refused to budge. "Wait," he hissed against her mouth.

She stilled.

"Just wait a minute," he whispered. His blue eyes gazed into hers, in them, a plea for her compliance. He was trying to stop her from being caught in the act, following Charmers. She breathed in his scent, masculine with a hint of something woodsy, and let her lips rest against his. For a crazy moment she was totally aware of him—the breadth of his shoulders, the warmth of his mouth, the feel of his chest beneath her palms.

Then he glanced to the side, and tracking his gaze, she saw Charmers walking down the street away from them. The stranger released her the moment Charmers disappeared from view.

"Just stay away from him."

Before she had a chance to protest or question him, he strode across the road, climbed into a battered pickup and drove away.

Betty stood on the sidewalk for a long moment after he'd gone, chest heaving as she fought to pull in air. Her heart was pounding and her legs felt wobbly, as though she'd been sprinting. She pressed her fingers to lips tingling from the imprint of the stranger's mouth. It was a bright, clear fall morning. Normally, the sight of the morning haze over the mountains would calm her, center her. The unexpected, close-up-and-personal encounter now made that impossible.

She made her way into work in a daze, only realizing she'd forgotten to buy pastries when she pushed open the door of the garage she was the part owner of, Under the Hood. Even though she was late, it was still early morning and the garage was quiet.

Her fingers shook as she peeled off her coat and hung it up. There was a noise from the back, and the smell of coffee hung in the air. Tracking across reception, she went in search of Alice.

The door creaked as she pushed it open.

"Hey," Alice turned from the coffee machine, clutching a cup. Her smile faded at one look at Betty's face. "What's happened?"

"Am I that transparent?" Betty sank into the nearest chair, put her head in her hands, and closed her eyes. Her mouth was dry and her body shook with residual tremors. She'd kept it together all the way here, but now...

Alice's hand landed on her shoulder. "To me, yes you are. Come on, out with it."

"I saw Charmers this morning from the window of the bakery. I dashed out after him—I had to find out where he was going so early in the morning, had to see if he was meeting someone."

"Oh God, you didn't confront him, did you?" Alice pushed back her white-blond hair, pulled a chair up and perched on it. Alice had been with her two weeks ago when they'd bumped into their customer Leonora De Witt and her new boyfriend in the weekly farmers' market. He'd introduced himself as Alexander Charmers, but Betty knew him as Alex Carlisle, the man she'd just about given up on ever finding.

In the three years since he conned her mother out of a sizable chunk of her savings, he'd barely changed at all. Face-to-face, he was smaller than she'd expected, less attractive. In fact, he looked much like any man in his late fifties would. Reasonably fit, with a touch of gray in his dark hair, especially above his ears. Moderately well dressed, but nothing to write home about.

Initially, there had only been the photographs of him with her mother, Christine, to go on, but a year later, with the help of a private investigator, she'd found a few more, culled from newspaper accounts.

"There would be no point in confronting him. He'd just deny it." Betty twisted her fingers together. "He's clever. A year after he conned my mother the FBI caught him, but he walked, and as my mother refuses to go public, I haven't got a leg to stand on. Not without evidence."

"I wish you'd go to the cops." It was a familiar plea. "You're becoming obsessed with catching this guy."

Betty straightened. Stared into her friend's eyes. "I can't let it go. That weasel stole from my mother. He even took the engagement ring my father gave her. I can't hand over responsibility to another group of men who are going to mess up catching him—I have to find some evidence that they can use to nail him." She gritted her teeth. "He's trying to do the same to Leonora, you know he is. How many other women have to suffer at the hands of this man?"

Alice nodded. "I know, I know. I just worry about you, that's all. So if you didn't confront him, what happened this morning?"

*He happened.* "I was following him. Discreetly, as always. There was no way he had any idea I was behind him on the street. And I saw him walk down between the dry cleaner's and the bank, so I was just about to follow him—"

Alice grimaced. "There are no shops to duck into down there, no cover."

"I didn't get that far. This guy just arrived out of nowhere and warned me off."

Alice's eyes widened. "A guy? Oh no, one of Charmers's men? Do you think he's onto you?

Betty shook her head. "I don't know who he is. But he's definitely not working with Charmers. I think he's after him too. He refused to let me follow, tried to get me to walk away because he was sure Charmers would come back." She rubbed her head. And he'd been right, hadn't he? If she'd followed, Charmers would have known she was following him.

Alice blew out a breath. "I imagine him

telling you to walk away didn't go down well." Her mouth twitched. "I wouldn't even want to tell you what to do."

"Huh." She wouldn't compromise for anyone, or anything. Three years ago she'd been in what had seemed like a serious relationship. But Jason hadn't understood her need to bring Charmers to justice—had wanted her to leave it to the professionals, to step back. He'd disagreed with her decision to hire a private investigator to try to find Charmers. Had told her it was a waste of time and money. *Her* money. When she'd discovered he'd gone behind her back and fired the private investigator, saying that she'd become obsessed in her search and branding her an amateur sleuth who didn't know what she was doing—she'd been beyond furious.

He'd insisted that as her man, he had the right to act in her best interests. Had told her it was time to let the past go, settle down, marry him, and have kids.

Faced with an ultimatum, she'd made the only choice possible. Had fired Jason from her life, and reinstated the private investigator.

"Well, you're right. I didn't take it well. I refused."

Alice nodded. "Called it."

"But then Charmers did turn around. And the stranger saw him coming back."

Alice gasped.

"So he backed me up against the wall and kissed me."

"He what?" Alice shrieked. "Some grubby, nasty stranger kissed you? Urgh, I just…urgh!"

"Well, to be honest, he wasn't exactly grubby or nasty. I mean, it wasn't that bad, and he didn't exactly, you know, slip me tongue or anything. He just pressed his mouth on mine, and shielded me from view. And the moment Charmers turned the corner, he let me go."

"What did he say?"

"He just told me to stay away. Then he walked off."

Alice shook her head. Stood up, and paced the floor.

"Well, that sure beats my morning."

*I've been so selfish focusing on my own problems.* Alice had been up since five taking Mel, the third partner in the garage, to the airport… "Of course, I'm sorry, I didn't even ask you. Did everything go okay?"

"Yup. I got Mel and Heath to the airport in plenty of time to catch their flight. They were so excited."

"I'm not surprised. If I was off to explore the Amazon for a month, I'd be excited too." An envious ache burned in Betty's chest, not for the trip, but for the fact that Mel had found the perfect person to share both the trip and a lifetime with, Alice's brother.

Alice pulled a bunch of keys from her pocket and handed them over. "Mel asked me to give you these. And I know she already told you, but she insisted I tell you again that Joe Carter is arriving at their house at six with the bed, and you're to be there to let him in."

"Yup. Got it." Mel had told her multiple times, and left her a text message as well. It wasn't personal, it was just the way Mel was, so organized she even color-coded her sock drawer.

---

*WHERE IS HE?* Betty checked her watch. It was almost quarter to eight, and there was no sign of the man. The morning's excitement had been followed by a day from hell where she hadn't even had time to stop for lunch. Again and again, her thoughts returned to the stranger she'd met that morning—wondering who he was and what he was doing in Meadowsweet. She shouldn't have had any reaction to his kiss, shouldn't have softened, but the remembered plea in his eyes and the warmth that had curled in her stomach as they'd stood so close had scattered her thoughts—disoriented her.

She'd been so distracted she was late leaving the garage to head out to Mel's house and had missed the chance to grab something to eat. Now, her stomach growled like a wild, angry bear. All she'd wanted was to let this guy in, wait while he reassembled the bed, and get to the store to replenish her empty pantry. By now, every store in Meadowsweet would be closed, and she'd have to resort to takeout.

Takeout was so unhealthy. Laden with too much oil, salt, and additives. Her stomach growled again. Betty stalked into the kitchen and threw open the refrigerator.

The interior light glowed bright. Every shelf was bare, except for a jar of capers and a sealed packet of beets. Betty pulled open the door to the freezer compartment. *Bingo.* Stacks of color-coded plastic boxes were lined up like miniature buildings. Green on the right, clear in the middle, and red on the left. She took out a green one and read the label on the top. "Vegetarian lasagna." A quick check confirmed that the green boxes were all vegetable-related. Vegetables were the angelic, low-calorie option, but Betty was in the mood for meat. Her growling stomach agreed.

She took a stack of red boxes out and laid them on the kitchen table, arranging them so she could easily read the labels. Beef casserole, spicy meatballs, barbecue pork. *Which to choose?*

"Hungry?"

Betty's heart pounded hard enough to burst. She swung around, and her startled gaze shot to the man who filled the doorway. A man with midnight-blue eyes.

*Him.*

Her hand fluttered at her throat. What on earth was the stranger from this morning doing here? Had he followed her?

"*You're* Betty?" His eyes scanned her face with an I-don't-believe-it look. He took a step forward, then another.

Everything in Betty rioted with the urge to escape. She eyed the doorway behind him and edged farther behind the table, putting solid pine between them. Her mouth was so dry it was as if she'd spent days crawling through the desert. *He knows my name.* She swallowed. "What are you doing here?"

"Calm down." As if realizing her agitation, he stopped. Held up his hands palms-out. "I'm Joe Carter."

"*You're* Joe Carter?"

"Is there an echo in here?" His hands lowered to his sides. The tension seemed to leave his shoulders and the corners of his mouth lifted in a smile.

Smoothing a hand over her hair, she glanced down at the table. A funny, fluttery feeling on seeing that smile replaced the panic she'd felt moments earlier. Unwanted awareness of him chased the tension from her body and filled it with warmth.

She rubbed the ache blooming at her temple. "Very funny." To her annoyance, her words came out husky-soft, rather than sarcasm-laced. "I've been waiting here for almost two hours for a carpenter to show up, and now you? If you're Joe, what were you doing grabbing me this morning?"

He avoided the question and looked past her at the open freezer door. "Looks like you were keeping yourself busy. Raiding the freezer, were you?"

*Huh.* "I was hungry. Someone kept me waiting." The only reason she would ever break into someone else's freezer was under desperate circumstances. "What are you, carpenter or…"

"It's complicated." He smiled, and once again attraction grabbed her insides with both hands and twisted. "But I have got a job to do this evening before we talk. I'm hungry too." A black eyebrow arched. "Maybe you and I could have dinner after I've assembled the bed?"

Faded jeans rode low on his lean hips and clung to his thighs. Above them, he wore a chunky navy sweater under a battered black leather jacket. Average, everyday clothing. But the breadth of his shoulders, the glimpse of tanned collarbone evident in the dip of the sweater's crew neck, were far from average or everyday. She scanned down. Work boots. Big work boots. *Big feet, big…* Cutting that thought off at the pass, Betty's gaze shot up to collide with his.

Amusement danced in his eyes. "Well? Like what you see?"

Betty put her hands on her hips. Raised an eyebrow of her own. This flirtation was getting out of hand—fast. She glanced behind him through the hallway to the front door he'd left open. The sky was darkening.

"I guess you should bring the bed in. I'll

show you where you can put it." She brushed past him, aware of a subtle extra swing in her hips as she strode to Mel and Heath's bedroom. "The bedroom is down here."

As she turned, his gaze snapped up to her face. "Great." He took a look in. "Could you help me bring it in?"

Part of her wanted to say no, but that would be childish. Alice and her boyfriend, Mark, were always raving about what a nice guy Joe was. She couldn't believe that Mark's friend was the same guy she'd met this morning. But the sooner he set up the bed, the sooner she'd get some answers. "Sure."

She followed him outside, picked up a couple of long carved pieces of wood, took them inside, and then returned for more.

It took four trips.

"The bed will take a while to assemble." Joe opened up his toolbox. "Why don't you go ahead and heat up dinner? Did you see something you liked?" He didn't look at her.

"I liked the look of the meatballs."

His gaze shot up to hers. A slow grin spread across his face, and with a wicked look he said, "I'm guessing you're talking about Mel's rather than…" He glanced down. At his crotch.

"Oh!" Betty turned her back, hiding her smile from his view. She compressed her lips to stop a laugh from bubbling free.

*I don't like him.*

While the meatballs heated, Betty made spaghetti and set the table. Who was she kidding? That crack about meatballs had lent Joe Carter a whole new dimension. Good looks were one thing, but good looks wrapped around a humorous center? Deadly. If they'd met under normal circumstances she'd be climbing aboard the flirt train, destination bed, with her sexy underwear stowed for the ride. But there had been nothing normal about the way they met— he'd been observing her following Charmers this morning, which meant he had to be involved, somehow. Her mind tumbled over the possibilities. Maybe he was a suspicious mark who was onto Charmers too. Maybe he'd been involved in one of Charmers's schemes.

She pressed her lips together. She couldn't let her guard down. Had to play this cool. Joe Carter was attractive, but he was hiding something, so he could pack away his grin and his innuendo—she sure wouldn't be playing.

When the meal was ready, she went to find him.

The bed was in place, and he was stowing his tools.

"Wow." The elegant bed was made of a light wood, with delicate carved spindles at the head and base. Rather than the traditional detailing that was found in such beds, the lines of the spindles were plain, almost Shaker. A modern classic. "That's gorgeous." She walked over and smoothed a hand over the curved headboard. "Did you really make this?"

"Yes, I did. It's made of beech." Joe snapped his toolbox shut.

"When Alice and Mark told me your work was good, they weren't kidding."

He smiled, obviously pleased with the compliment.

"Dinner is ready if you are."

"Great. I'll just wash up."

Betty went into the kitchen and started to put their meal onto plates. She was driving and so was he, so she didn't open a bottle of wine, just filled a jug with water from the faucet. She couldn't remember when she'd last eaten alone with a man.

Joe strode in. "I'm seriously hungry," he admitted. "I missed lunch." He pulled up a chair, and Betty put a plate down before him.

"So who are you?"

"You know who I am." He picked up a fork. "Joe Carter. Mark's friend. A carpenter contracted to make Mel and Heath's bed." He started to eat.

"Yeah, sure." She injected as much snark as possible into her words. "I think we're past that, don't you?" Elbows on the table, she leaned forward over her dinner and glared at him. "Who are you really, and what are you doing in Meadowsweet?"

# TWO

Ever since he walked into the house and come face-to-face with the mysterious brunette who'd filled his thoughts all afternoon, Joe had been trying to work out how exactly he was going to handle this.

He'd spent the last two years trying to trace the con man whose intricate web of identities had allowed him to vanish without a trace once he'd walked from custody on a technicality. A technicality Joe was responsible for. A dormant account he was watching had shown an ATM withdrawal in Meadowsweet. The financial crimes unit at the FBI had discovered payments from Alex Claybourne's account to an Alec

Corben, and Joe had been positive that Claybourne and Corben were the same man.

Corben's withdrawal in Meadowsweet was a tenuous lead the bureau would be reticent to follow up on—even if Corben and Claybourne were the same man, there was nothing to suggest he'd actually settled in the tiny town in the Blue Ridge Mountains. So Joe'd taken annual leave and boarded a plane to find out for himself.

He'd asked around, but found no sign of the mysterious Corben. He had been on the last day of his vacation when he'd seen Claybourne walking down the main street arm in arm with an attractive older lady as though he didn't have a care in the world. Discreet inquiries had revealed a new name: Alexander Charmers.

Elated, he'd talked his boss, Bond, into letting him stay in Meadowsweet to investigate further. And today, he'd been forced to break cover the moment Betty stumbled into the investigation.

"Well?" Betty crossed her arms and stared him down. Her brown hair tumbled in waves over her shoulders, a strand or two slipping beneath the neckline of her white shirt as if caressing her creamy skin. Unlike most women he met, she didn't seem to go for makeup much, judging by the light spattering of freckles over the bridge of her nose.

Her eyes were an unusual shade of brown; he guessed some might call them tawny or something, framed by long dark eyelashes. He hadn't been able to stop looking at her wide, generous mouth, even when she was sniping at him. Fear had flickered in her eyes when she'd seen him in the kitchen earlier, quickly masked, but he'd recognized it instantly. When she'd tilted up her chin, met his gaze square on, and questioned him, admiration for the smooth courage she displayed had been his overwhelming emotion. After surprise so intense it verged on shock that Betty Smith and the woman he'd started to call Nancy Drew in his head were one and the same.

He rubbed the back of his neck. "I could ask you that question."

"I'm Betty Smith. Friend to Mark and Alice, one-third owner of the Under the Hood garage," she parroted in an echo of his earlier answer to her question.

*Smart-ass.* "So why are you tailing Charmers?"

"Who said I was tailing Charmers?" Her eyes narrowed.

*It's going to be a long night.*

Joe pushed his plate to one side. "Look, we can do this two ways. We can continue to bullshit each other, or we can just be goddamn honest." His jaw was clenched so tight it ached. He refused to break eye contact, or even blink.

"Fine," she huffed. "I was following him."

She might not have noticed him before, but her curves were so familiar he could pick her out in a woman-only marathon. "You've been following him for two weeks." She wasn't a professional, that was for sure. Her clumsy attempts at trailing Charmers had been driving him crazy. She kept a reasonable distance, but dashed into doorways every time Charmers turned, as though she'd been watching one too many cop shows. And when Charmers and Leonora had gone for coffee last Tuesday, she'd lurked on a table outside with the collar of her raincoat turned up, reading the damn newspaper, for Chrissake.

Her eyes were open so wide the whole white was visible. "How do you—"

"I've been following him for longer." He blew out a breath. There was no alternative. His cover was in tatters now; he'd have to confess. "I'm an undercover FBI agent."

"You're FBI?"

Joe nodded. "I have him under surveillance, and the last time I checked, no agency allows garage owners to run their own private investigations, so what gives?"

Her throat moved. She reached for the slender gold chain around her neck and rubbed it between her fingers. "Charmers conned my mother, Christine Tremaine, three years ago. He took her money and ran. I tried to find him, but it was as if he'd fallen off the face of the earth."

"Three years ago?" Joe's blood quickened. He'd slipped the FBI net two years ago—there'd been no cases they knew of before that. "Did your mother report it?"

"No." Betty chewed the corner of her bottom lip in a way that fractured his focus, made him wonder what kissing her for real might be like. "I tried to get her to, but she was embarrassed about being taken for a fool, and wanted to keep it secret. I employed a private investigator right after, but there was a misunderstanding and he abandoned the trail." She frowned. "By the time I got my investigator back on it, he'd disappeared. It took a year, but we eventually saw a picture of him in a newspaper. He'd been using a different name, and the FBI had caught him running a scam on another woman. I don't know what went wrong, but they let him walk. I couldn't believe it when I saw him in Meadowsweet, using yet another alias. And starting to do exactly the same scam on another unsuspecting woman." Her hands curled into fists.

"I know." Joe knew from bitter experience, because he'd been the FBI agent who screwed up. He'd been so focused on catching Charmers he'd allowed the chain of custody on key evidence to be broken. This time, everything would be done by the book, and Charmers would have no chance to escape.

He couldn't blame Betty's mother for wanting to protect her privacy; the list of Charmers's actual victims was probably double the number reported to the FBI, which made his movements so difficult to trace. "What name was he using?"

"Alex Carlisle."

Alexander Charmers, Alex Claybourne, Alec Corben, all names familiar to Joe and his team, and all the same man. Excitement skittered along Joe's nerve endings at the unrecognized name Betty had provided. *Alex Carlisle.* He needed to notify the team as soon as possible and crunch that name through the system.

"Where does your mother live?"

"In the Hamptons."

There were no recorded victims in the Hamptons. Perhaps, like Betty's mother, they'd neglected to report the crime. Rich society would be easy pickings for a man like Charmers, impossible to resist.

"She warned her friends off him, but didn't go into specifics. He was living in a beach house that he said he'd bought. Of course, once he disappeared, the truth came out that he'd rented it." Betty wrung her hands together. "Now he's trying to con Leonora. Who knows how many other lives he's ruined over the years?"

"Maybe dozens. Maybe hundreds," Joe said. "Your mother must come forward and make a report."

"To the FBI?" Her tone was dismissive. "They'll just screw it up again."

"So your plan is to make a citizen's arrest or something, is it? You're going to get him in an armlock, wrestle him to the ground, and handcuff him?"

Her mouth tightened. Her eyes flashed. "I'm not an idiot. I planned to gather evidence. I picked up a Styrofoam cup he'd thrown in a trash can in the park, but then I saw you can't get prints from that—"

Curiosity made Joe interrupt. "Where did you learn that?"

"*CSI.*"

"The TV show?"

She nodded and spoke rapidly. "Yes. Styrofoam's no good. Paper is better, but then you've got the problem of maybe picking up stray prints, so glass is best. They were having lunch outside a restaurant last week; I managed to pick up his glass after they left and before the server removed it."

He'd followed Charmers and his date, had missed her stealing a glass from the table. Joe held back the eye roll and puffed out a frustrated breath.

"You couldn't get it dusted for fingerprints though. Unless you have a…"

"I have fingerprinting powder and a brush. I've found latents." She looked ridiculously proud of herself. "Of course, I don't have access to AFIS, but…"

"IAFIS," Joe corrected. "In the FBI, we use IAFIS."

"Oh." She stilled. "I didn't know that."

There was a ton of stuff she didn't know. She probably thought a computer zipped through all the available prints and…

"I thought we could load the fingerprints into AFIS."

She grinned and corrected herself, "IAFIS, and then it would find a match—"

"It's not as easy as you see it on TV, you know." He rubbed the ache blooming at his temple. "Where did you get the fingerprinting powder?"

"I have my sources. Anyway, I put the glass in a plastic bag. So it wouldn't be contaminated."

"Great." A glass with someone's fingerprints, dusted by a kid's fingerprinting kit, wouldn't be of any use, but she'd worked so hard, he couldn't bring himself to point that out. "What else is on your agenda to catch him then?"

"I want to establish a paper trail, get access to his bank statements, that sort of thing." She gazed at the floor. "He stole my mother's engagement ring."

"You don't expect to find it, do you?"

The truth was written all over her face. She had hoped to find it.

"Was it worth much?" The moment the words left his mouth, he realized his mistake.

Betty rolled her lips together, compressing them into a tight line. "To my mother, it was priceless because my father gave it to her. Dad didn't have much money, but she came from a rich family and my grandmother gave it to my father to propose with. It's one of a kind. Probably worth tens of thousands."

If they'd known about Betty's mother, his investigators could have used the considerable resources at their disposal to find that ring if and when he'd sold it. Could have tied Charmers to the sale of stolen property. The loss of a valuable lead rankled, making his tone sharp.

"It'll be long gone. We need your mother involved," he insisted again.

"She won't. I told you—she doesn't want her humiliation made public. I tried, Joe. She said the only thing worse than what happened would be everyone knowing about it. And if it went to trial she'd have to testify, wouldn't she?"

Witnesses were always reticent to come forward. The shame that they had been taken in held them back. A member of the general public was no match for a confident trickster. They used the subtlest methods to squeeze money out of their marks. Charmers had even faked a medical condition with one victim—she'd agreed to pay his medical expenses, and had taken him as far as the door of the hospital for treatment. He'd taken the money, walked in through the hospital entrance, and kept walking through the exit at the back of the building.

Betty looked tired, suddenly—beaten—and for a moment his heart softened.

"Okay. I understand where your mother is coming from. But you can't go after Charmers on your own. He looks harmless, but he's anything but. I have resources you don't. I'm on top of it, I've got a trace on his cell, and I want to get inside his house to plant a bug there, too, and search for evidence. Leave it to me."

"No." She tossed her hair back, her answer instant and unequivocal. "I can't do that. I'm sure you're competent but…I just can't."

"So no matter what I say, you're going to keep following him?" *She's going to be the death of me.*

She sat up straighter. "Yes."

Everything had to go by the book. This was no game for amateurs—the last thing he needed was Betty playing detective. He'd worked too long and too hard to allow that to happen.

"You're interfering in an investigation, do you understand that? If you don't butt out, he'll slip the net, probably with Leonora's money in his back pocket." He stood and pushed back his chair. "If I see you anywhere near him again, I won't be kissing you, I'll be handcuffing you."

"Oh, you'd like that, wouldn't you?" Her full lips pursed.

She flicked her hair back and stood too. "I think it's time for you to leave." Fire blazed in her eyes, and despite the fact that she was as irritating as sand in a swimsuit, he did want to handcuff her. And kiss her, too.

SHE HADN'T BEEN able to sleep—had tossed and turned until the break of dawn trying to work out how she was going to nail Charmers. Joe Carter's involvement on the scene was an unforeseen problem she had no solution to. He'd been adamant that she shouldn't be involved, but there was no way she was leaving Charmers's capture to someone else.

When her alarm blared, she almost turned over and ignored it, but couldn't. There was work to do, so she splashed water on her face, downed a large cup of coffee, and drove to Under the Hood.

Car maintenance classes usually happened during the week, after the day's work was done, but today was different. It was Saturday morning, half past nine, and thirty-two intrepid women had turned out for the free "Change your tire yourself!" class. Two cars were parked outside Under the Hood, and in front of them were two identical tables with a variety of tools set out on them. In front, Alice and Betty addressed their students.

"So, who's had a flat tire?" Alice asked. About half the women raised their hands. "And what did you do?"

Eva, a barista in the local coffee shop, called out, "Showed some leg till someone stopped to help!"

Alice nodded. "And it usually wasn't another woman who stopped to help, was it?"

"I had a flat last week, and I had lots of women stop to commiserate, but none of them knew where to start," Eva admitted. "That's why when I saw this course was on, I decided I had to get my butt out of bed and get down here and find out how to do it myself. I don't want to be a helpless female waiting for a white knight to ride up and save me, and I'd like to be able to help out a friend if it happened to her."

Instead of overalls, Betty and Alice had chosen to wear regular clothes and heels to do the demonstration. They wanted to show that any woman, armed with the knowledge and the proper tools, could change a tire. If they were dressed as mechanics, the impact of the message they were trying to get across would be diluted.

Step by step, Alice read out the tasks from the second handout, which detailed how to change the tire. In perfect unison, like a well-oiled machine, they picked up items from the tables and attacked the job at hand.

When they were finally finished, both cars had new tires. Along the way, women had asked questions, learned answers, and relaxed enough to chat with one another. All in all, it was a great morning.

Betty sidled up to Alice as the women swarmed around the tables, chatting and picking up tools. "Are we still on for this evening?" There was only a week to go before the Meadowsweet Vintage Rally, a yearly event that Mark had decided to enter this year, with Betty going along as navigator. Over the past few weeks, it had become a routine for Betty to join Alice and

Mark for dinner, after which Betty and Mark took a drive out around the countryside.

The three-day rally covered a vast distance, with timed stages, and they were working on improving their communication and time around the first stage. Every night, Betty clutched a map and stopwatch in the passenger seat, and Mark drove as she provided commentary, reminding him of the twists and turns that were coming up. When he'd originally entered the race, it was with the intention of taking Alice as his navigator, but that had fallen apart fairly quickly. Nothing destroys a couple's relationship quicker than driving together.

Leonora and Charmers had entered too, and she was determined to get close to Charmers on this trip.

"We sure are. I can't guarantee what sort of a mood Mark will be in, though. He's out at his sister's today—she has him installing a security light above her front door."

Mark's sister, Susan, had taken one of their car maintenance classes. She was a strong, independent woman.

Like siblings the world over, Mark and Susan irritated each other without measure. They argued about everything, but deep down, when it mattered, they were there for each other.

"She could easily pay an electrician to do that, rather than ask Mark," Betty said. Mark worked long hours; he didn't need his weekends cut into.

"She could, but she mentioned to Mark that she needed one, and of course, he volunteered." Alice smiled. "He said it was an easy half hour up a ladder, and she'd be crazy to pay someone to do it when he could without breaking a sweat."

Her cell buzzed, and Alice pulled it from her pocket.

"Speak of the devil…"

While Alice took the call, Betty walked to the table and talked to their class. "Okay everyone. Are there any more questions?" The group shook their heads. "In that case, we're done. Thank you all for coming today."

Alice finished up her call and joined Betty. The group clapped and swarmed around them, thanking them for taking the time to teach them the basics.

Alice looked pale and worried. "That was Mark."

JOE WAS EATING lunch when the phone rang. He put the oversize sub down, swallowed, and answered. "I need a favor." Joe's only friend in Meadowsweet, Mark, sounded exhausted. He'd met Mark the first week he arrived in Meadowsweet, and enjoyed his company. The lawyer was open and honest, and despite Joe's reticence to get close to anyone, they'd become friends.

"I was putting up a security light outside Susan's house yesterday, and I fell off the goddamn ladder and broke my arm."

"Oh, you're kidding me." *Who'd joke about a thing like that*? Joe rubbed at the back of his neck and reworded. "That's desperate, man. Was it a bad break?" He'd broken his arm once. Or more accurately, had it broken for him. A memory burned through him of his father shoving him aside as he tried to get between him and his mother. Alcohol sometimes made the old man's eyes unfocused, but not this time. He'd stalked toward Joe's mother with cold intent evident in the hard, clenched line of his jaw and the anger blazing in his eyes. When he'd raised his hand,

Joe had pushed his mother aside and taken her place.

"It's not too bad." Mark's voice jerked Joe back to the present. "It was a clean break, and they've put on a cast. The problem is I'm driving in the rally next week."

"Oh yeah." They'd talked about it often enough. Mark was fanatical about his car, and taking it on the vintage rally was something he'd been really looking forward to. "I guess you'll have to ditch that. There's no way you can do it with your arm in plaster."

"Well, that's the thing." Mark paused for a moment. "If it was just me, sure, I'd pull out. But we've been promoting it as the team from Under the Hood. Alice, Mel, and Betty have done a lot of publicity about the race. A lot of clients have gotten involved, and there's a gang of clients ready to wave us off. There's a whole social media campaign in place. Being involved with a vintage rally is a great way to get the word about the garage out, and more than that, it's fun. From Meadowsweet, the rally continues up into the mountains.

"It's a three-day rally. The first night there's a dinner with a charity auction. For the second, there's a black-tie event and a lavish casino night where all the profits also go to charity. Tuxes, ball gowns, the whole deal. The last leg brings the drivers back to Meadowsweet on Friday. The Hunter's Moon Festival happens Friday night, and there's a huge party. The community really gets into it."

"So what's the plan?"

"You know me. I don't let anyone get their hands on my baby. Most people around here have no clue how to use a stick shift, never mind driving an MG competently. Each team must be one man and one woman, so I need a male replacement. There's only one person I would consider. And that's you. I know it's a big ask."

A memory of one of their previous talks floated to the surface. "Isn't Betty your navigator?" He was flattered that he was Mark's first choice, and even though three days and nights cooped up with Betty keeping his hands to himself held little appeal, he wished he could say yes, and help a friend out. But he couldn't. He had to stay on Charmers, couldn't risk letting him out of his sight for a moment. "I don't know…"

"Would you come to dinner tonight? To discuss it? It would mean a lot to me," Mark said.

Rejecting Mark's proposal over the phone was impossible; he'd have to turn him down face-to-face. "Okay, I'll be there."

He heard Mark blow out a relieved breath. "Great, come over about seven, and we'll run through everything over dinner."

Joe hung up and called his boss, Michael Bond. The previous night he'd passed on the information about Charmers's Carlisle identity and he was eager to find out if they'd tracked down bank financial records.

"We hit pay dirt, Joe," Michael Bond said. "From what we can tell, Alexander Carlisle is his real name. The paper trail is clean and clear. We've identified deposits that match the amounts and dates of some of his previous scams, and a couple of checks from other women who haven't come up in our inquiries before."

Adrenaline flooded Joe's veins. "Is one of them Christine Tremaine?"

"Yes, that's your contact's mother, right? He took her for a hundred and twenty-five grand."

Joe whistled. "That's a hell of a lot of money. I hope we can persuade Tremaine to testify."

"She has to testify. The only other way we can tie him to the account is if he makes another deposit we can trace."

"What about the bank? Can't they identify him?"

Bond made a noise somewhere between a laugh and a snort. "It's an offshore account. Set up online. There was no human interaction, no one to see his face."

"So we need to catch him in the act—see him run with someone else's money. Or get proof positive that he and Carlisle are one and the same."

"Yes. There's one other thing." Bond's voice lowered.

"I know you want to get this guy, but we have a problem," Bond said. There was the rustling of papers. "Leonora has a son—Josh De Witt. Currently serving in Afghanistan. Due to finish up his deployment in two weeks. He'll be heading straight home to Meadowsweet."

The clock was ticking. Once Charmers knew that Josh De Witt could visit his mother soon, he would take what he could and get out of there.

"He must be aware of this and he'll be trying to finalize the con," Bond said. "We have to wrap and get a team in place for extraction this weekend. You have to get him on the hook before then."

Joe's hands tightened into fists. "I need more time—"

"Time you no longer have, Joe." There was regret in his boss's voice. "This guy is clever, he specializes in small-time scams, and the largest amount he's managed to con out of anyone is the sum he managed to get from your informant's mother. We need to either catch him in the act now or persuade the Tremaine woman, or someone else whose money has turned up in the account that he might have conned, to testify. Be careful. If he realizes you're onto him, he'll run again."

# THREE

At six forty-five, clutching a bottle of pinot noir by the neck, Joe climbed out of his truck and started walking to Mark's door.

A flash of lights from a car parked a little way up the street caught his attention—then the inner light went on to reveal Betty, scooping the air with her hand in a come-over-here wave.

He sidetracked to her and opened the passenger-side door.

"We have to talk," she hissed urgently. "Get in. I don't want anyone to see us."

Joe held back a grin and did as she asked. "You mean Charmers?" Mark and Alice's house was on the outskirts of town in an area that

Charmers didn't visit, and they were following him, not the other way around.

"It's always wise to be cautious. There's no need to draw attention to ourselves."

"So, what's up?"

"It's about the rally," Betty spoke fast. "Alice phoned me and told me you're going to stand in for Mark, and we need to get some things straight if we're going to be spending days and days together—"

"I'm not going to do it. I need to keep focused. Need to keep watching."

Betty grinned. Mischief sparked in her eyes. "Oh. So you're going to stay here?"

"Like I said…"

She flicked a strand of chestnut hair that had fallen in front of her face away. "I'm guessing that you don't know as much as you think you do about Charmers's whereabouts for the next few days."

Joe was instantly alert. "What do you know?"

"Say please." She looked different tonight. A section of her hair was fastened up at the back, in a half-up, half-down style that emphasized the curve of her cheekbones. He peered closer in the dim light cast by a streetlamp. Her eyes looked different too, sort of mysterious. Maybe it was the dusky shadow on her eyelids, or mascara. There'd been a TV ad a while ago with a sexy voiceover talking about smoky eyes. Yeah, she was definitely going for that.

Her low-cut black top had some sort of silver thread woven through it, making it glitter as she moved. The air was scented with her perfume, something warm and spicy. Joe rubbed the back of his neck. "Please." His voice sounded strained to his own ears.

"Leonora and Charmers have entered the rally. They've entered Leonora's Rolls, and we have it in the garage right now, getting it serviced ready for the trip. If you want to keep an eye on him, you'll have to take Mark's place."

She looked so damn pleased with herself, Joe's head ached. "I told you, I don't want you involved."

"You don't have any choice. Believe me, the thought of being stuck in a car with you for days doesn't set me on fire either, but we both want the same thing and we're going to have to work together to achieve it."

"I work alone." In Mark's house, the upstairs light went out. They were going to be late. "We should go in." He reached for the door handle.

She touched his arm. "You can't on this one.

There have to be two people in each car, and there is no way I'm letting you switch someone else into the navigator's seat. Mark and I have been practicing for ages. If you want Charmers you're going to have to work with me. Like it or not."

Having a hothead like Betty along added an element of unpredictability into the mix that made nerves clench in his stomach. She wasn't a trained agent, and what's more, she seemed determined to hold her ground and not back down no matter what the circumstances. Part of him admired her for her tenacity, recognizing it as a trait that they shared.

Completing this assignment, bringing Charmers to justice, was all that interested him. He couldn't let anything get in the way of a satisfactory outcome. The imminent arrival of Josh De Witt on the scene made it imperative he stay with Charmers and Leonora on the rally—whatever was going down would happen soon. She was right; he'd have to work with her. He breathed in deep and exhaled through his mouth. "Okay."

"There's one more thing." Her tongue swiped across her bottom lip. "He saw us—you had me pretty well shielded, but he would have registered you were kissing someone." She rolled her lips together and swallowed. "So we'll have to pretend to be a couple."

———

HE STOOD by the car as she grabbed her bag from the back and locked it. Took her arm as they walked to the front door. In black jeans and a black shirt open at the neck, he was vitally male, and her insides flip-flopped at his nearness. *I'm going to have to kiss this guy.* That wasn't going to be a problem—but making sure she didn't start wanting it for real could be.

"He probably didn't even notice us," Joe said. "I really think you're overreacting."

"You said yourself he suspected me of following him." Betty's jaw clenched. "We were so busy staring at each other, we don't know what he did when he walked past us. He could have checked both of us out. Anyway, a couple is less likely to draw attention than two strangers working together."

"Says who?"

"Says everyone." She shot him a glance.

"You definitely watch too many movies."

And doubtless read too many books. In

reality, there was nothing unusual with a driver and navigator on a rally who weren't involved romantically—her relationship with her previous driver, Mark, was totally platonic, wasn't it?

"If he noticed us, he'll think we're a couple already," Betty insisted. "If we only start behaving as if we're hot for each other at the starting line, Mark or Alice could blow our cover. So we should make it look as though we're getting involved from here on in so there's no possibility of tipping him off."

"So try to look as though you like me." Joe reached out and tucked an errant strand behind her ear. Her skin tingled at his touch and she breathed in deep, trying to center herself.

"Well, try to act likeable. Otherwise we won't be fooling anyone." Betty plastered a smile on her face as the door swung open.

"Hi!" Alice opened the door wide and spied the bottle Joe held out. "Oh, pinot—perfect!" She stepped close and kissed him on one cheek and then the other, then did the same to Betty. There was a question in her eyes. An ooh-what's-going-on-here question. "Did you two come together?"

"We arrived at the same time," Betty said.

"Hi!" Mark walked up the corridor behind Alice. "Come on in."

Mark's arm was in a sling, and he sported a bruise on the side of his face.

"Ah, poor you." Betty reached for Mark's free hand and squeezed it. "That must hurt. Were you high up the ladder when you fell?"

"High enough," Mark said. "Luckily I landed on grass. I came down hard on my whole right side, but nothing else is broken. I'm taking the rest of the week off work, and Alice is going to drive me back and forth next week. Business is slow at the moment so I can do a lot from home."

"You've only just gotten over that punch to the jaw, too." Two weeks ago an irate husband, furious at his wife's divorce lawyer, had stormed into Mark's office. Mark restrained him quickly, but not before he received a punch to the jaw.

"Yeah, I've been attracting a lot of bad stuff recently. Let's get something to drink." They followed him into a large room set up with a seating area at one end and a dining area at the other. "What do you think of the new table and chairs?"

Betty walked over and ran a hand over the smooth wood of the oval table. "Gorgeous."

"All Joe's work," Mark said. He picked up an opened bottle of wine, but Joe took the bottle out of his hand.

"I'll do that." Joe filled four glasses and handed them out. His fingers brushed her hand as he did so, sending a flurry of shivers up her arm. "I have the other two chairs you ordered made, and I'll deliver them tomorrow."

"The minute I saw the table in the Furniture Nook, I just knew it would be perfect here," Alice said. "Your work is selling really well there."

Joe nodded. "They've put in an order for a replacement set. I'm pretty busy."

She didn't know much about him, except for the fact that he was an accomplished carpenter, an FBI agent, and damned sexy. Betty took a sip of her wine. Finding out more was a priority.

"I'll just check on dinner," Alice said.

"I'll help." Betty followed Alice into the kitchen and closed the door. "Okay, there's a problem." She grabbed Alice's arm and pulled her to the window on the opposite side from the closed door. "I didn't get a chance to tell you this morning but Joe is the kissing guy."

"Joe—"

Impatience made Betty's voice sharp. "Yes.

Joe. He's the guy who stopped me following Charmers."

"God. Does he know about Operation Charmers?"

Betty shook her head. "No. I've told him about my mother, and that I'm trying to find evidence, but nothing more than that. He's an undercover FBI agent, and wants me to keep his secret, so you can't tell Mark."

"I wasn't going to."

"It gets worse. We have to pretend to be a couple because Charmers saw us together." Her head ached with the complexity that Joe's involvement had brought to the situation. She'd had a plan, and now that plan was in danger of being compromised. She wasn't sure what to do, what way to turn. The experience with her mother had taught her caution—Charmers had slipped through the net before.

"So you're going to have to kiss him for real, and stuff?" Alice brightened. "I think you and Joe would make a great couple. Maybe when all this is over, you could be a couple for real."

"Alice, for goodness' sake…"

"Mark thinks you'd be good together too. He's been pushing me to introduce you. That's why he took me out the other night, so you could meet him at Mel's when he delivered the bed."

Matchmaking was in Alice's blood, but the fact that Mark was just as bad was a surprise. "Mark was trying to set us up?"

"What can I say, he's a romantic. Like me." Alice opened the oven, poked at a casserole, and closed the door again. "I know you're not thinking of romance right now, but keep it in mind. He's a nice guy."

"A nice guy who's lying to his friend," Betty retorted. "There's no way I'd ever be involved with a man like that, a man who hid his real identity." Her mother's experience with Charmers had made her cautious of men who said one thing, and hid their true intentions.

"You're not exactly being honest either," Alice said. "And if he's undercover, he has to lie; he can't just come right out and let everyone know what he's up to. Anyway, he's told you now, there's no reason not to trust him."

"I'm only giving him information at the moment on a need-to-know basis." She'd shared everything with her ex, and he'd made the decision to interfere and fire her private investigator. Joe might well decide to take matters into his own hands, to squeeze her out—there was no way she'd blindly trust him.

"Dinner's ready. Help me carry, and we'll eat."

---

IT WAS good to get a home-cooked meal. Alice surreptitiously cut Mark's meal into bite-size pieces and the glance that passed between them as she handed it over was full of warmth and love. What would it be like to be so close to someone else? Joe'd always been a loner. He'd had a couple of relationships, one with a member of the bureau, but neither of them had survived. He'd let himself believe it was the pressure of work that had sounded the death knell, but both of his previous partners had broken up with him for the same stated reason. He didn't share himself. Didn't let them know the man inside. Didn't reveal his past.

Sharing a nightmare was supposed to steal its power, but he couldn't stand the thought of receiving pity for the hell his father had put him and his mother through. And even though it wasn't logical to blame a child for the beatings his mother had sustained, shame still lived deep in his heart that for so many years he hadn't been able to help. Hadn't been able to make it stop.

"Have you always wanted to be a carpenter?" There was an edge to Betty's question, an undertone as she was well aware that carpentry wasn't his main means of making a living.

"I sort of fell into it by accident," he answered honestly. "I learned some in school, did it as a hobby mostly. I didn't apprentice with anyone, but I collected tools, and took a few night classes."

The shelter that he and his mother moved into had nothing except what people gave them. The furniture was secondhand and shabby. Often badly repaired. The only other man allowed in the shelter was the janitor, a man Joe'd thought of as old, even though he must have only been in his early sixties. He taught Joe how to renovate the furniture in his workshop in the back garden, which held his collection of tools. Being there, working on restoring what was broken, gave Joe some kind of peace. If only his broken mother could be repaired so easily.

"You're very good at it."

"I enjoy it." The feel of the wood, the

satisfaction of creating something with his hands, had always been fulfilling. "I like creating." He placed his palm flat on the dining table, remembering the hours of care and attention he'd poured into the task while building a credible cover. His day job wound him tighter than a drum, but working with wood unraveled him. "The cabin is a perfect place to work."

"You and that cabin are a match made in heaven," Mark said. "It was a stroke of luck I was in the Realtor's that day…"

"Mark's family roped him in to help with a relative's property," Alice explained. "He was what, your great-uncle?"

Mark nodded.

"So, Mark's great-uncle was too old and infirm to live in the cabin any longer, and he had a love of carpentry, and a fully stocked workshop. He didn't want to sell—I think the old guy wanted to believe he'd be able to go back to live there someday—but leaving it empty wasn't a good option," Alice explained.

"So I was at the Realtor's—seeing if I could find someone to rent it," Mark said. "And there was Joe, a carpenter looking for somewhere to rent. It was the perfect solution to both of us. We worked out a temporary lease on the cabin—he gets a workshop out of the deal, which is perfect for his job, and I get to keep fishing in my favorite stream."

"Yeah, they say they're fishing, but I reckon they just sit there drinking beer," Alice teased. "Mark took Joe out to see the cabin that day and they've been friends ever since. Once we saw Joe's work, we decided to buy the table. He's working on chairs to match."

"I went for the fishing, and stayed for the friendship."

"And the beer," Joe added. He really liked Mark, and wished he didn't have to keep so much hidden from him. When this assignment was over, he'd have to confess to Mark that his life was way more complicated that it appeared. God knows if their friendship would survive that.

"I love fishing." Betty smiled.

"You do?"

Her smile widened into a grin. "Yeah, I do. I used to fish with my dad." Her eyes sparkled.

"Well, for the whole experience, you'd have to like drinking beer too."

"I do. I love beer."

"She sure does. I could tell you some stories

about Betty and beer." Alice collected their plates. "We've had some pretty wild nights. Some even including dancing—"

Betty went pink. "Oh c'mon, Joe doesn't need to hear—"

"What? Tell me." The way Betty was trying to put Alice off was damn cute. "If I invite you over are you going to frighten the fish with your singing or what?"

Betty's lips twitched into a smile. "It was just one time…and Alice and Mel dared me…"

"You should have seen it," Mark added.

Curiosity spiked. "Out with it, what happened?"

Betty laughed. "One too many beers, 'Single Ladies' blaring out of the sound system in the bar, and a table made for dancing on…need I say more?"

Mark and Alice laughed along with Betty at the memory, and Joe smiled. She was so different in this fun and flirty mood. Their interactions so far had been tense, a complex mix of fighting and plotting. It was good to spend time with her flip side; maybe the rally would be fun after all. With dinner finished, the conversation turned. "I guess we should talk about the race," Mark said.

"I'm going to do it."

Mark blew out a breath. "Thank God. I really didn't want to put my baby in anyone else's hands."

"Hey, I thought I was your baby," Alice teased.

Mark grinned. "You're my sweetheart." He leaned over to kiss her cheek, but she shifted so that their mouths met.

"I'll get the maps." Betty pushed her chair back and walked to the sideboard, picked up a sheaf of papers, and brought them to the dining table. Her movements were jerky, as though, like him, she'd been affected by Mark and Alice's closeness.

"Would you guys like some coffee?" Alice asked.

When they all replied they would, she glanced at Mark. "Want to help me?"

"Yeah." The look Mark slanted Alice's direction hinted there was more in the kitchen than making coffee to interest him. "You guys start, we'll be back in a minute."

The moment they were alone, Betty spoke. "They've gone to the kitchen to make out; they're not going to be back for ages."

The way she looked at him made something kick inside Joe, something spark. There were golden glints in the depths of her tawny eyes, a tiny mole just above her full mouth. He breathed in her scent with every breath. "I like your perfume."

Her breath hitched, and her pupils expanded. Her skin looked soft, and she was close enough to touch. He reached out a hand and stroked his fingers over her cheek.

"What are you doing?" Her voice was breathy, but she didn't move away; instead, she leaned into his touch.

Joe trailed his fingers down, over her neck. "Getting used to being close to you."

Her lips parted, and her eyelashes fluttered. "There's no one watching us, Joe. We don't have to pretend." Her eyes darkened, and the air seemed to spark between them.

He battled against the overwhelming urge to kiss her. "You're right."

"Although I guess we could practice, make sure we look as though we've kissed before." She leaned close, stroked the side of his face, and looked at his mouth.

There was nothing but the feel of her fingers against his skin, the uneven rise and fall of her chest as he stared at her downswept eyelashes. Awareness narrowed, focused like a laser on her face. The curve of her cheekbone, the soft bow of her upper lip. When Betty breathed out, tilted her jaw upward, and put her lips on his, there was no way in hell he could resist.

She'd been in his arms before. He'd pressed his mouth to hers in anger, in an attempt to keep her safe—but this time was different. This time, he closed his eyes and let himself feel. He teased her lips with his tongue, felt reason dissolve. Her hands smoothed over his neck and speared into his hair, demanding he come closer, give her more. A little voice inside urged caution, but he didn't listen—couldn't listen while his senses rioted at the touch of her, the scent of her, the taste of her.

Joe's heart thundered in his chest as the kiss deepened. The spark had flared into a full-on forest fire, one he had no chance of dousing.

BETTY'S MIND had been battling her body ever since she'd sat down next to Joe for dinner this evening. His easy banter with Mark, warm appreciation of the meal before them, and ease at her friends' home had seduced her into a fantasy that they really were just there to spend time with mutual friends. She'd let herself daydream about touching him, had wondered what his strong arms might feel like around her, what his broad chest would feel like beneath her fingers.

From the first moment she'd seen him, she'd been fighting an overwhelming attraction. She'd managed to quash her instinctive response to his nearness until he'd started to talk about making furniture with passion in his voice. Relaxed, in the company of friends, he'd become accessible, possible hot fling material. And once Alice and Mark had gotten touchy-feely, she'd been whisked up in a lust tornado.

They sprang apart at the sound of footsteps and rattling cups.

Reason returned like a splash of ice-cold water. *What have I done?* She'd made the mistake of not only indulging her passionate side, but actually starting to like him. Had turned off her mind and let her body do what it wanted. For a wild, thoughtless moment, she'd abandoned reason, had forgotten that she couldn't just blindly trust—couldn't let down her guard without risking the success of her mission. The mission to catch Charmers.

"I'll open the door for Alice." She jumped up and dashed for the door.

Being in the close confines of the MG day after day while staying detached would be darned near impossible.

# FOUR

Alice and Betty met up the following morning in Under the Hood. Over coffee, Alice said, "There was an email this morning from Mel. She managed to send it by the satellite phone."

"Was it full of tales of her adventures?" A whole month in the Amazon sounded like heaven, even if they had bugs and beasts to deal with. "I bet it's really beautiful."

"She sounded happy," Alice said. "Apparently Heath is being really attentive and taking some fantastic pictures."

"So no reminders of things we should be doing?"

"A couple." Alice grinned. "But we have them all covered, so they aren't worth mentioning." She refilled her coffee and looked innocent. "What time are you meeting up with Joe this evening?"

Alice hadn't seen anything the previous evening, but seemed to possess a supernatural sense when it came to flirtation or attraction of any sort. Of course the fact that Betty could barely string two words together when Alice and Mark had come in with coffee, coupled with the extremely mussed nature of Joe's hair and smear of pink lipstick on the corner of his mouth, was probably a dead giveaway.

She and Mark had shown Joe the practice route on the map last night, and then she'd agreed to meet him tonight to drive it. As Mark was clearly exhausted, to her relief they'd called it a night at that point and gone their separate ways.

"You do like him, I can tell." Alice pulled up a chair and sat. "You haven't dated anyone since Mike; I think you should jump his bones."

"Alice!"

"Don't pretend to be shocked—if you were the one giving me or Mel advice, you'd be telling us exactly the same thing, you know you would."

There was no arguing with that. "Well okay, I find him attractive. Who wouldn't? And I'm sure he can be charming if he puts his mind to it, but he likes to tell me what to do, and as you know, I hate that with a vengeance." It was normal for the three partners of Under the Hood to microanalyze the early stages of one another's crushes. Like therapy, only cheaper with no possibility of censure. Talking about Joe —well, it was different. Their attraction had been pretty much mutual and instant, uncontrollable. She hadn't meant to kiss him the previous night, but had been drawn to him like a wrench to a magnet.

"You say you always want to do everything yourself, but you work well with me and Mel— you delegate and share responsibility fine with us."

Alice was right; when it came to decisions about their company, she trusted the others implicitly. Not only were they invested in doing the best for Under the Hood, but also the bond among them was stronger than blood. They were closer than sisters. "That's because I trust you guys."

Alice tilted her head to the side and tucked a skein of white-blond hair behind her ear. "I know how important Operation Charmers is to you, but you might have to let someone else in.

You might have to drop your guard and trust Joe."

*I have to work with him, but I sure don't have to trust him, not unless he proves himself worthy.*

Betty glanced at her watch. "Leonora will be here soon."

"The Rolls is ready," Alice said. "Shall I bring it around?"

Betty shook her head. "I'll get it. I bought a bugging device the last time I was in Chesapeake. It'll only take me a couple of minutes to install it..."

Alice frowned. "I don't think the garage should be involved."

"I'd only do it with Leonora's consent...I was going to suggest it to her this morning."

"That might be illegal," Alice insisted, "and I really don't want the garage involved in anything hinky."

"Okay, I guess we're done with her car then." Frustration burned in Betty's chest. She knew Alice was right, and it was vitally important that she didn't do anything that might let Charmers escape on a technicality again, but it was just so difficult to be working in the dark all the time.

She wanted to keep a closer eye on Leonora,

too—more and more often she was meeting with Charmers alone, which could be dangerous. She needed some form of protection, some backup.

The buzz of the doorbell heralded the arrival of a customer.

"That will be Leonora," Betty said.

"I'll bring the car around and then make myself scarce."

"Come on in," Betty greeted Leonora and led her to the sofa in the back of the reception area. "How's everything?"

"Well it's okay, but Alexander seems very anxious to take things to the next level." Leonora swallowed and looked around nervously. "I've told him we have to have separate rooms for propriety's sake during the rally, but I don't know how much longer I can hold him off when we return to Meadowsweet."

Betty hated to see Leonora under pressure. "I should never have suggested this…"

Leonora held up a hand. "You didn't suggest it. We decided together, remember? The first time I met him at our canasta night, I was totally charmed. If we hadn't bumped into you when he took me to the theater a couple of nights later, who knows what would have happened." She shuddered. "Actually, I know exactly what would have happened. If you hadn't taken me to one side and told me your suspicions—hadn't shown me the picture of your mother and Alexander together, well, I might very well have been his next victim." She squared her shoulders. "I'm not a fool, and I damn well resent being taken for one. You were looking out for me. Just as my son Josh would have if he were here instead of serving in Afghanistan. Did I tell you that he's coming home? He'll be back for my birthday, a week after the Hunter's Moon Festival—I can't wait to see him.

"Oh," Leonora said, as if suddenly remembering. "I heard that Mark broke his arm, but that can't be right, can it? I mean you are still in the race, aren't you?"

"Of course," Betty replied; there was absolutely no way that she would abandon Leonora. "He did break his arm, but we have a replacement. In fact, it works out even better than having Mark involved, because the new driver, Joe Carter, is an undercover FBI agent hunting Charmers too."

"I should meet up with him then," Leonora said.

"Not yet." Betty leaned forward. "I haven't told him about your involvement. He thinks you're just an unwitting victim, let's keep it that way for now, okay?"

———————

BETTY PULLED up outside Alice and Mark's after work. Joe's pickup was parked outside. She grabbed her bag containing the map and stopwatch from the passenger seat, walked to the front door, and rang the doorbell.

Alice answered the door. "Hi." She turned and called behind her. "Betty's here."

Mark and Joe walked out of the living room. Joe looked up. "Hi, Betty. All set?"

"Yes."

"She's all fueled up and ready to go." Mark handed over the keys to the MG. "Have a good drive—no need to hurry back. Why don't you stop off for dinner?"

Betty'd come straight from work and had planned to make herself something when she got in, but Joe nodded at Mark's advice. "That's a good idea," he said. "We might just do that."

Her head buzzed with questions as she climbed into the tiny car and strapped on the seat belt. Joe pushed the seat back as far as it would go, pretzeled his long legs getting in, and tested out the pedals. He spent a few moments fiddling with the mirrors and fastening his own belt before he turned the key in the engine, put her into gear, and...stalled it.

The words that came out of his mouth would make a nun blush.

Betty smothered a giggle. "You know they're watching from the doorway, don't you?"

"Yes, I do." He shot her a glance, ran through the procedure again, and this time they pulled out of Alice and Mark's drive. "I reckon I stalled it because I was so aware of Mark watching. He was giving me one hell of a talk about how to look after his baby before you arrived."

"He does love this car," Betty agreed. "You're saying you're not just a terrible driver then?"

Joe smiled. "I'm not a terrible driver. But I haven't driven a stick shift in a while."

He was working the gearshift like a pro now, weaving the little car through the end-of-day traffic as though born to it. He obviously loved to drive. "So, the first stage is up into the mountains?"

"Yes. Take a left up ahead."

He complied.

"Okay, the starting line will be just up ahead —parallel to the bank. There are thirty-five entries this year, and the cars leave from the starting line one by one. The road is closed to general traffic, so we don't have to worry about that."

"So I guess we want to get ahead of the pack as quickly as we can."

"It's not that sort of a race," Betty explained. "Have you even seen a vintage rally before?"

"It's a race. How difficult can it be?"

Betty puffed out a breath. He had a learning curve to climb, straight up. "I think we should rethink this evening. Let's go and have dinner and I'll talk you through it, then we can go for a drive to get you used to the car." She gestured ahead. "Take a left—we'll grab a burger at the diner."

Once they were seated and had ordered, Betty pulled a number of items from her bag and laid them out on the pitted Formica tabletop. "Okay, when Mark and I say we have been driving the first stage of the route, we've actually been driving what we *think* might be the first stage. We won't know the actual route until just before the race, when they give us one of these."

She put a route book down on the table before them, angling it so both could see.

Joe took it. "What are the numbers down the side?"

"The diagram on the left shows each step of the race, and the numbers show the distance. The navigator is handed this at the beginning of the race, and I have twenty minutes to plot the route onto the map." She pulled out a map and put it on the table too. "Then"—she rooted in the bag again and retrieved a small card—"our time is recorded on this card by an official and we start driving. I'll be telling you where to go…"

Joe raised an eyebrow. "Which you'll be good at, I bet."

"I will." She grinned. "And more importantly than that, I'll be telling you how fast or how slow to go." She pulled out a handful of pens and a stopwatch from her bag. "There will be control points along the route that we need to arrive at on time. We can't be too early, or we lose points, and we can't be too late."

"Define too late."

"Five seconds too late will earn us a penalty point. As will five seconds too early."

Joe groaned. "That's going to be impossible."

"Difficult—but not impossible." She almost felt sorry for him—she and Mark had been practicing driving and timing, but there was no time for Joe to become nearly as expert as Mark. "We're not trying to win this," she explained. "We entered the rally to raise the profile of the garage and to take part in the community. There's no disgrace as long as we finish. The rallymeister has timed each stage and set the time targets, and we have to stop at each control point and get our time recorded on the card before continuing."

"We have three days of this?" He looked tortured.

"With stops for lunch and dinner. It won't be so bad." She looked up as the server arrived at the table with their food. "Let's eat and then you can drive a stage and I'll time it." She picked up the items from the table and stowed them in her bag.

THE FOLLOWING days followed a similar pattern. Despite her forebodings, Joe turned out to be a quick study and an accomplished driver. He paid attention to her directions, and by the time their third outing came to an end, they were coming close to hitting the time target for the stage.

Eating at the diner with him had become routine too.

"So I think we're all ready for tomorrow, or as ready as we can be." She forked in a mouthful of apple pie. He was sitting next to her, rather than across the table. It made for more intimate conversation, with less chance of being overheard. She pitched her tone low anyway. "How's the surveillance going?"

He didn't answer, just stared into her eyes as though she was the only person in the room, a look so intimate her insides turned to water. The blue shirt he wore made his eyes even bluer. He'd undone the top couple of buttons, and rolled up the sleeves to reveal strong, muscled forearms dusted with silky hairs. She caught his scent in the air with every breath, clean, masculine, and distinctly him. For a moment she was thrust back to the first moment they met. The moment he'd curled his hands around her shoulders and pressed his mouth against hers. He'd been a stranger, but even then she'd been far from immune to his proximity.

His hand covered hers, and he leaned in to

trail a leisurely kiss against her cheek. The brush of his mouth against her skin sent shivers down her spine. Her eyelids closed and she turned her face to claim his mouth.

"Excuse me," the waitress said. "I'll just take these away for you."

"Thank you." Joe leaned back. *Of course*. The move, the kiss, was to maintain their cover. To give the impression to everyone that they were a couple. He doubtless had seen the waitress's approach, and wanted to make sure that their conversation remained private too. Her stupid heart's beating faster was irrelevant.

When they were alone again, he scooted closer into the corner and pulled her with him. "I've been generating a rumor around town for the past few days. That I'm not just a carpenter —I'm a guy who was made redundant and given a large payout. I asked the Realtor if there was any possibility of buying Mark's uncle's house. For cash."

"Oh my God, Melly McCarthy." She shook her head. "She's really indiscreet—"

Joe grinned. "I know. Alice said the same thing. That she'd tell everyone."

"It's going to take more than a rumor that you have enough money to buy a house to bait

Charmers," Betty said, wishing he'd edge away a little, stop scrambling her senses with his nearness.

Joe nodded. "There's a charity auction the first night of the rally, and a casino night the second. I think I can throw around enough money to catch his attention."

"Catching his attention is one thing, but it will take time to build a relationship with him— to get him to offer to invest your money for you. He's cautious; he's been dating Leonora for ages. He won't open up until he feels he can trust you. Maybe we could confide in Leonora, get her on our side and…"

"No." Joe was adamant. "This isn't one of your detective novels. Leonora's no Miss Marple. The more people we involve, the more likely it is that a mistake will be made."

Betty's heart dived. He wanted to run every single element of the investigation—thought he had all bases covered and certainly wouldn't approve of the steps she was taking behind the scenes. The bureau had let Charmers walk before. Much as she wanted to, confiding in him was too risky.

"It's dangerous, too," Joe added. "Charmers could be dangerous when crossed."

"Not all women are delicate flowers who need to be protected at all costs."

Joe's jaw tightened, but he said nothing.

Betty puffed out a breath. *Maybe all FBI agents have hero complexes…* "So you build a relationship with him, get him to trust you over the rally, and let him know you have money to invest. In time—"

"I don't have time. If we don't act quickly, we may lose him."

# FIVE

The cars were lined up along Meadowsweet's Main Street. The route books had been handed out, and Betty and the other navigators sat at long tables next to the starting line, plotting the route from the instructions onto their maps.

The rally organizers had arranged a bus to transport everyone's luggage to each night's stop, so all they had to worry about was supplies for the day. Betty had taken care of that too. The tiny backseat held a cooler with drinks and snacks, and she had mounted a tray on her side of the dashboard to hold the route book and map.

Joe glanced over and watched her work. She wore a denim shirt with a large pocket over her breast, which held highlighters and pens. Her chestnut hair was pulled up in a high ponytail, and glinted in the sunlight. There was a tiny wrinkle between her eyebrows as she expertly traced the route, then broke off to highlight certain portions of the route book.

If things were different, spending three days driving through the mountains with her at his side would be fun. They'd reached an easy understanding—a mutual respect over the past few days—and after he'd confessed his plan to catch Charmers they seemed closer, a team.

She glanced up. Found him. Then picked up the sheaf of paperwork and started to walk his direction.

"I'm ready." She went up on tiptoe, and kissed him smack on the mouth.

Shocked, Joe just stood there. Her mouth was soft. The scent of flowers drifted from her hair, from her warm skin.

"Put your arms around me. We're meant to be a couple, remember?" she whispered against his mouth. "Charmers is watching."

Damn. He'd wanted to kiss her again ever since that night at Mark's house. And now that he had to, it was impossible to pretend to himself it didn't mean anything. He snaked an arm around her, pulled her close, breathed in her summery, lemon scent, and kissed her back.

She tasted just as he remembered. Her arms went around his neck, and she pressed herself against him, giving Charmers and the entire population of Meadowsweet a show they wouldn't soon forget.

Joe's head swam.

"Woo-hoo!" A cheer from somewhere in the crowd broke the spell.

Betty pulled back. "That should do it." She grabbed his hand. "Let's get our card stamped and get going."

Joe looked around. The sidewalks were packed with enthusiastic spectators. Alice and Mark stood at one side, Alice holding up a makeshift banner she'd painted with Go, Joe and Betty! in giant letters, while Mark and some of the garage's customers waved little flags with Under the Hood's logo—a '50s housewife holding a wrench—in the air.

Alice was grinning—more than likely that "woo-hoo" had come from her. She jiggled the banner and Mark gave him the thumbs-up.

With a weak smile, Joe returned it and climbed into the MG. He squeezed his hands around the leather steering wheel, drove up to the start, and waited while time control wrote their start time on the time card.

Betty grabbed two bottles of water from the cooler and dropped them on the floor at her feet. She clutched the map.

"Ready?" She turned to him, a wide smile on her face.

"Ready." The moment time control handed her back their time card, he gunned the engine and they were off.

Betty kept up a running commentary as they sped down the road. There were spectators all the way down Main Street and on the road out of town.

"Wow, this is great."

Betty laughed. "Isn't it? Mark said the rally was popular, but I hadn't expected everyone to turn out for us." The staff had come out of every store and coffee shop along the route. Even the customers from the salon came out, some of them in curlers or with their hair stacked in shiny foil layers, and waved as they went past. Betty waved back, with delight on her face. "I love this. We should do it every year."

*Every year.* Joe's hands tightened on the steering wheel. If he were just a carpenter, if he really lived in Meadowsweet, there wasn't anything he would enjoy more. The joy that glowed from Betty was infectious. When she'd kissed him, he'd let himself imagine they could be together—had let himself get swept away in her crazy fantasy. "Watch your speed," Betty tapped the speedometer. "And take the next left ahead. They're very sneaky—they plotted a route we haven't practiced. It's going to be tricky." She pulled a calculator out of the bag on the floor and started tapping keys. "I'm trying to calculate our speed until the next control point. I need to calibrate our speedometer with the rallymeister's too. There's bound to be some variation."

She was totally focused on the task at hand. Probably hadn't given a second thought to that kiss, when it was all he could think about. Joe forced himself to concentrate on the road. "How many control points?"

"Just two in this stage." She gazed out the windshield. "Here comes that left."

He took it, and she ticked it off in the route book.

"Okay, we're going straight for five miles." She glanced across at him. "This is fun, isn't it?"

"Yeah." She was having such a great time. Her hair bobbed every time she looked down at the map, and then up at him or out the window. He couldn't help but get into the spirit too. "When are we stopping for lunch?"

"You hungry already?" She grinned. "You ate enough breakfast."

Before the race, the competitors had been treated to a full breakfast in the Meadowsweet Hotel. "Who could resist those pancakes?"

"Not you, obviously." She laughed. "I don't know where you put it. If I ate that much I wouldn't fit my butt into this car."

He was still thinking of her butt when they rounded a bend to see an old Corvette with a cloud of smoke coming from the tailpipe.

"They're in trouble. We should stop."

Betty shook her head. "Can't. It's against the rules to stop to help another driver. We have to leave that to the support team. They're following."

"How far back?"

"At the end," Betty admitted.

Joe hit the turn signal, then passed the stricken car. The navigator was shouting at the driver, who climbed out and slammed the door hard. Looking in his rearview, Joe saw him kick the tire.

"Ouch. Promise you won't go crazy if we break down?"

Betty was bent over the map as the road snaked in a long curve around the side of the mountain. "Promise. If we break down, I'll fix us."

IT WAS A GLORIOUS DAY. The sun wasn't harsh and glaring, like the rays of summer, but bathed the road ahead in a golden glow that painted the dappled undergrowth. There were no distinct clouds in the sky, merely the occasional film of white, as if sprayed by a fine airbrush. Betty's mood soared like the birds overhead. She cranked down her window a tad, breathed in the crisp air, and let the pure joy of being out in the elements overtake her. "This beats being in the office any day." She glanced across the car. "In your real life, is carpentry just a hobby, or did you used to work as a carpenter?"

"I used to make furniture, and fitted kitchens," Joe said. "But it's a cutthroat business if you're doing it for money. There are a hell of a lot of carpenters out there, and there's no way to compete with the ready-to-assemble sellers. I wasn't interested in selling something below what it cost me to make it, and I couldn't live on what I made for my work, so I moved on."

"To the FBI."

"Yeah."

"It's not a natural progression from carpentry." She examined his face for a trace of emotion, a hint to what had propelled him into this different career. "Although I guess in both you spend a lot of time alone."

"I'm not really a people person. And I guess I like bringing people to justice. There are a lot of con men out there. Charmers is the tip of the iceberg." His mouth tightened. "Not everyone is capable of the detachment involved in tracking someone. They get emotionally involved, and being invested in the outcome makes them reckless, liable to screw up."

His words struck a note, deep within. She'd do anything to get Charmers. The changes he'd wrought in her mother had ignited an anger inside that was all-consuming. "He really did a number on my mother. Before him, she was sort of naive—she believed the best of everyone. I was away at college—I thought she was safe." Her chest ached. "Now she doesn't trust easily. She's guarded. I hate to see that in her."

"It wasn't your fault." Joe glanced over. "You know that, don't you? I've looked into a lot of his previous scams. Charmers is a master at deceit. Even if you'd been around, you wouldn't have suspected anything."

Her heart tightened. Despite his words she did feel guilty, did in some way feel responsible. There had been only the two of them for years now. She'd been so anxious to get on with her own life, she had been casual about her mother's. Christine had asked her to come home to meet her new boyfriend, and she'd been too busy. Maybe if she'd made the time…

"Don't blame yourself."

Ahead, the road snaked to the left. Betty checked distances and ticked off the latest section on the map. "There's a right turn half a mile ahead. Then we should be arriving at the first control point. We'll stop and hand the card out of the window to be time-stamped, then we're on our way again." She checked the stopwatch, then the speedometer. "We're running a couple of minutes late, up the speed a little."

As many of the cars and owners were older,

there was nothing taxing about the first morning's drive. The rally was more like a huge Sunday outing where enthusiasts took their cars out. By the time they arrived at the end of the first stage, the sun was high in the sky, and she was more than ready for lunch. They got their time recorded on the card, parked the MG, and walked across the grass to the front door of the restaurant that was hosting their lunch.

A large sign in the lobby proclaimed, "Welcome Meadowsweet ralliers! Lunch is served in the MacKenzie Room." They followed the arrow pointing the way into a large dining room. A buffet lunch was set up on tables on the right, and clusters of smaller tables were dotted around the room.

"There's Leonora." Betty grabbed Joe's hand. "Come on."

"Hi, Betty," the older woman greeted them as they approached. She waved to some empty chairs. "Do join us."

Charmers wore a polite smile. His gaze flickered to her, to Joe, and then to their linked hands. Betty pulled out a chair. "Leonora, Alexander, I don't think you've met Joe?" Nerves shimmied in her stomach being so close to

Charmers. "The first stage was easy enough, wasn't it?"

"It was for some." Leonora darted a look at a couple just entering the dining room. "Ed Fleming and his wife had some problems."

Betty followed Leonora's gaze. The couple driving the smoking Corvette didn't seem to be talking. The driver was scowling and his wife was patently ignoring him. "That's Ed Fleming?" She'd heard that the reclusive writer lived in Meadowsweet, but hadn't met him. "I love his books."

"I don't know his work," Joe said.

"Yes, you do," Leonora replied. "Everyone does. I've never read them, but I watch the TV series they made. It's called *Crime Bite*."

"It's damned good." Betty leaned close to Joe. "You know the way I love crime shows? Well, *Crime Bite* is my favorite."

"Is that the one about the vampire private investigator?" Joe grinned. "The one who seems to remove his shirt at every single opportunity?"

"He's a serious investigator." She couldn't help grinning. The show was great, with lots of clever twists, but he was right. The lead actor did strip every episode.

"Oh yeah. Obviously." Joe smiled.

"I'm starving," Charmers said. "Can I get you something from the buffet, darling?" He placed a hand on Leonora's, focused his entire attention on her, in a way that he must at one stage have done to Betty's mother. Betty gritted her teeth. *What a creep.*

"Let's all go." Leonora stood.

Over lunch, they made casual conversation about the race and the challenges ahead. Charmers discussed politics, the state of the economy, but never once veered into personal territory. All Joe's attempts to deepen the conversation led nowhere—the older man was charming, attentive to Leonora, yet reserved. His dark eyes never strayed from her face, and although he smiled politely at Betty's jokes, he didn't laugh. He was a difficult nut to crack.

The coffee had been served and drunk— there was no excuse to stay.

Betty unhooked her bag from the back of her chair and stood. "See you at dinner."

---

THEIR TIME WAS RECORDED on the card again, then they were off.

"This next stage will bring us up to the

ridge," Betty said, examining the map. "It's only seventy miles, but the road winds and the speed limit is low. The rallymeister has estimated two hours in all for this stage." She marked the route book. "You want to drive straight for three miles, then turn left just before what looks like an old farmhouse."

"Okay." Joe concentrated on the road ahead. Charmers was canny and cautious. He had no reason to trust either of them, and was obviously reluctant to. Leonora, though, had been friendly. As one of Under the Hood's long-term customers, she knew Betty well, but he'd been pleasantly surprised that she'd invited them to join their table for lunch, and asked them to join her and Charmers for dinner as there were plenty of participants she seemed to be friends with.

Making the first meeting had been easier than he'd thought, but Charmers's natural caution would be difficult to overcome—especially in such a tight time frame.

"Here comes the farmhouse—take the turn to the left just before it." Betty ticked off the direction with her pen. "Straight on from here. Slow down a little. Keep our speed to about forty."

"Right." He edged off the gas and breathed deeply.

"I wanted to be a private investigator when I was a kid," Betty said. "I always thought it would be so glamorous, creeping around, trying to catch bad guys. I used to make invisible ink with vinegar and write secret messages everywhere."

A long-buried memory surfaced. He'd only been six or seven, and even though his father must have been living with them at that time, he was absent from the memory—making it a good one. "I did the same. My mom found me crying in the kitchen clutching a knife. I remember the look on her face—she thought I'd hurt myself." He glanced over, couldn't stop the smile that spread across his face at the memory. "The only thing I'd hurt was an onion. I chopped it to bits and mashed up the pieces in a bowl, trying to make ink from onion juice. My eyes itched, so I rubbed at them, making the whole thing worse."

She winced. "God, onions are so horrible! I can't even peel one. Rubbing your eyes must have been agony!"

He checked the speedometer. "So you watch crime shows, enjoy making invisible ink, and tracking people—why the hell did you become a mechanic?"

"My father." She ticked off a point on the chart and reached into the back to ease the lid off the cooler. "Water?"

He shook his head, so she pulled a bottle out for herself, and took a sip.

"My dad was a mechanic. My mother's family was rich, and my father worked for them. They came from totally different backgrounds, but they loved each other until he died."

There was a trace of sadness in her eyes.

"I'm sorry about your dad. How long ago did he die?"

"When I was a kid. My mother's family was sure he was just after her money. They told her she wouldn't receive a penny of her inheritance unless she divorced him. She never did." Her smile was warm as she remembered. "Dad was always able to provide for us. And my mother used to say all the money in the world wouldn't be enough to separate them."

"How did she manage after his death?"

"They relented. Gave her access to the trust they'd put her money into. She doesn't care much about money—she bought a house in the Hamptons because she's always loved the ocean."

"So you followed in your father's footsteps."

"When I wasn't being a private eye, I was with him, tinkering under the hood of a car." She grinned. "They always talked about how they first fell in love. Mom wrapped her first car around a tree on its first outing, and brought it to him on the quiet. She wanted him to fix it and not tell her parents. He did, but not until he'd given her hell for driving too fast. He insisted on going out with her four or five times to check her driving. He made her crazy." She laughed. "He was so good at making her laugh. After he died, she didn't laugh for a long time. For years."

"He sounds like a great guy."

Betty glanced over. "He was. I miss him."

"I know how that feels." Even though it had been years, he still missed his mother, never more than this time of year. The anniversary of her death was coming up, and that always stirred up memories. Mostly bad ones—but today he'd remembered something long forgotten. A time when they'd been happy. "Charmers took her for a lot of money."

"Yes." Her voice was no louder than a whisper. "He took more from her than money. He led her on, lied to her, and stole her faith in humankind." Her fingers clenched into fists. "I hate him for that."

Charmers had done more than that; his actions had affected Betty too—must have added a layer of mistrust and disillusionment to her open, trusting nature. Joe's fingers clenched around the steering wheel. The damage was done. It was important he stay focused and detached, but the thought of bringing Charmers to justice and renewing Betty's faith, seeing her happiness, added an extra impetus to succeed. To do the job right.

Betty's happiness mattered.

# SIX

The afternoon faded, and by the time they approached the final control point there was a chill in the air.

They were high in the mountains now. On the way up, the sun had set, painting the sky every shade of blue and pink in the process. The mountains were heather mauve and dark denim blue in the curved dips between the peaks. As night fell, birds scattered, settling on their roosts for the night. Betty had pointed out the fluttering outlines of bats against the night sky as they left civilization behind and headed deep into nature's heart. This land was so different from the smog-filled cities Joe knew. Here, they were one with nature. He had even rolled the window down to breathe in the cold, crisp air—until Betty's protests had forced him to close it again.

They stopped at the final control point and got their time recorded, then parked outside a large wooden hotel that looked more like a giant log cabin than anything else. Smaller cabins were attached to it on both sides, forming a square with a central courtyard garden. A table of drinks was set up at the entrance.

A waitress smiled as they walked over. "What can I get you?"

"Champagne sounds good," Betty said.

"Make it two." Joe turned to Betty.

"So that's it for today, huh?"

"Yes." She took a sip. "There's a meal at seven thirty, and we don't start off again until ten tomorrow morning." She rotated her shoulders and tried to stretch her aching back. "I don't know about you, but I'm dying to get out of these clothes."

Joe smiled. Raised his eyebrows.

Heat flooded Betty's face. He was only teasing, but still the idea held a certain appeal.

"I'm dying to climb into a hot bath. *Alone.* To ease my muscles."

"Yeah, I know, I was just messing with you." Joe drained his drink. "Let's go check in."

Reception handed them keys, and gave them directions to their rooms, which were in the main hotel. Joe followed her to her room, then when she had unlocked the door, turned away. "I'll come get you at seven thirty, then."

---

JOE'S LUGGAGE and laptop were stacked neatly on a luggage rack in his room. They would be spending two nights at the hotel, so he unpacked his suit and tux, and stacked his spare clothes in the drawers.

The room was dominated by a huge four-poster bed. Joe tested the mattress, then strode in to check out the bathroom. Along the back wall was a claw-foot tub, and to the side a small shower enclosure. His body ached from being stuck in the car all day, and the thought of a long, hot bath was appealing, but he needed to check in with Bond—find out if they'd had any luck tracing any of the new names in Charmers's hidden bank account—so a shower would have to do.

He stripped off his clothes, left them lying on the floor, and climbed into the shower.

The complimentary bottles of shampoo were

tiny. And the soap was barely bigger than a pack of matches. Joe did the best he could with what was available. At least the shower pressure was good and the water hot. As he soaped his chest, his thoughts turned to Betty, next door.

Right about now, she'd be luxuriating in a huge tub. *A tub big enough for two*. There had been a flash of awareness earlier when he'd teased her about getting naked. And the way she'd kissed him this morning had been above and beyond what was needed to maintain the pretense of a fake relationship. All day he'd tried to keep on track, not just in the race, but in his head. The car had been full of her scent, and the way she glanced across the close confines of the car at him, the intimacy of working closely with someone with a shared goal, had eroded his defenses.

The more time he spent with her, the more he liked her. For years he'd been alone, hiding his true identity and purpose from everyone. God knows he hadn't wanted to reveal himself to her, but the circumstances of their meeting had forced him to, and the time they'd spent talking had brought them closer.

She felt guilt for not looking out for her mother. He'd never shared the truth of his background, the guilt he felt every day that he hadn't been able to get his mother away from his father sooner. Once upon a time, he'd wanted to fight back, show the old man what it was like to suffer under the fists of another.

But that would have made him and his father the same, so instead, he'd channeled his fury into law enforcement. Into standing up for women made weak by love of the wrong man.

His history had seemed too deep, too personal to share with anyone before—but he had the feeling Betty might understand.

She was getting under his skin. What would it be like to have more, to actually have a real relationship with her when this was all over?

*One thing at a time.* Joe turned off the faucet and wrapped himself in a towel. Catching Charmers must be his entire focus; he couldn't afford to jeopardize that by being distracted, no matter how compelling the distraction.

---

TONIGHT FELT LIKE A DATE. She'd luxuriated in the hot bath until her fingers and toes had turned pruney, couldn't stop thinking over the day's events. But instead of stressing over Charmers, her mind had been filled with thoughts of Joe.

His voice. The way he didn't talk much, but somehow made each word matter. When driving, his movements were economical, but sure. She'd never had to repeat a direction—they worked together like a finely tuned machine.

A thread of attraction linked them. Tonight would be even more so, as they pretended to be a couple once again. Maybe Alice was right. Maybe she deserved to have a fling with him. It didn't have to be forever—he had a life and a job to go back to once Charmers was in custody, but every time she thought of him, every moment in his company made it more difficult to resist him, and for the life of her, she couldn't remember why she even should.

Then she remembered. He only knew half the story. That she was determined to get Charmers. He didn't know that she and Leonora had planned to bring him to justice by trapping him, catching him in the act. Taking things further without revealing the truth would be dishonest, and time to catch Charmers was running out. They had to wrap this operation up fast.

She pulled open the wardrobe doors. The

red silk chiffon, or the gold Azzedine Alaïa? She ran a hand down both and decided on the red. Cut daringly low with a sweetheart neckline and a swatch of fabric that curved over one shoulder, it was a shut-up-and-look-at-me dress. One she'd bought in a mad moment for far too much money because she hadn't been able to resist it, but had never found an opportunity to wear. Luckily the bodice was discreetly lined, because it was cut too low to allow the wearing of a bra. She slipped it over her head, smoothed the expertly draped front, stepped into high gold stilettos, and turned to check the back view.

The gold watch her mother had given her on her last birthday was next—and she checked the time as she fastened it. Three-quarters of an hour to go. Time enough to curl her hair and arrange it with the jeweled clasp she'd borrowed from Alice. And to go all-out with makeup for the first time in what seemed like forever.

*Yup, it sure feels like a date.*

When the knock came at the door forty minutes later, she was ready and waiting.

The sight of Joe in the doorway stole her breath. Like her, he'd dressed up for the occasion. The slate-gray suit fitted perfectly, and he wore a snow-white shirt and a silver-gray silk tie. Freshly shaven, with his hair slicked back from his face to emphasize the sharp planes of his cheekbones and the blueness of his eyes, he made her heart race.

His gaze swept her head to toe, then returned to her face. His pupils expanded, swallowing up the blue. "You look beautiful." His voice was deep and husky. "Really beautiful." For a moment, time stood still. The air seemed to thicken, to charge with words unsaid and dangerous emotion.

Then he reached for her hand, and brought her knuckles to his lips.

Betty's legs felt weak as sensation flowed through her. "You look beautiful too." Pulling him inside her room, pressing her mouth to his, and ripping off his tie and shirt to run her hands over the broad expanse of his chest was an errant thought that she itched to follow. *We have a job to do.* "We should go."

"Yes." He released her hand and stepped back, looked away, and broke the spell.

Joe linked his arm through hers as they walked. Once inside the ballroom, he released her, but kept his hand at the curve of her spine as they joined Leonora and Alexander at their table. She couldn't take a step without being aware of him. Circular tables set with linen tablecloths and sparkling crystal glasses filled the dining room. The room was full of couples, filled with the murmur of many voices speaking, yet they could have been alone, so attuned to him was she.

Leonora smiled. "I love your dress—is it a Pamella Roland?"

Trust Leonora to know her designers. "It's a couple of seasons old, but yes, it is."

Joe filled her glass with wine, and then his own.

The rallymeister and the race organizers sat at a table on a makeshift stage, rather like the head table at a wedding, and once everyone had taken their seats, the rallymeister stood and tapped his glass with a knife.

Silence descended.

"We've had a great first day, everyone," he said. "We've tallied the time cards, and I have winners' jerseys for the driver and navigator who are in the lead at this stage." He looked down and consulted his notes. "Flora and Mac Jackson, would you come up here?"

The room applauded as Flora and Mac made their way to the stage to claim their jerseys. "Each day is timed separately—the team that does best overall will be the ultimate winner, but everyone has a chance to excel at the end of each day's stage and claim the winners' jerseys," the rallymeister said. "Tomorrow is another day —so good luck everyone. I'm sure you're all hungry, so I won't keep you from your meal any longer. We'll continue with the auction when we've all eaten."

He raised his glass. "Here's to the end of the first day!"

The meal was delicious. Thinly sliced beef and tiny roasted potatoes with butter-glazed peas and baby carrots, followed by an airy lemon mousse and fresh strawberries.

"So what's the route likely to be for tomorrow?" Joe asked.

"You know the area better than me, Leonora," Betty said. "But I know we are returning here tomorrow night, so I guess we could be looping around Hainsville and then back by the river road?"

Leonora considered for a moment. "That's one way, or they could have plotted a route farther into the mountains—around by Crystal Falls. There's a road that doubles back through there somewhere."

"I guess we'll just have to wait and see." Joe

covered Betty's hand with his. "Have you ever competed in the rally before, Leonora?"

"Oh yes." She brushed a strand of her short, silvery hair back from her face. "But not for years. My husband loved the rally. This is the first time I've done it without him, though." Her smile looked forced. When she picked up her wineglass, her hand trembled almost imperceptibly. "I think I'll freshen up before the auction begins." Her eyes flashed a plea Betty's direction.

Obeying it, Betty responded. "I'll join you."

They left the men at the table and made their way from the crowded dining room.

On the way to the bathroom, Leonora tugged at Betty's arm and jerked her head in the direction of an empty room off the lobby. "I don't want to be overheard," she hissed as they hurried inside.

"What's up?"

Leonora couldn't stand still. She paced back and forth in the silent room.

"Alexander mentioned an investment opportunity this afternoon in the car. He said he knew a company that was going to float on the stock exchange."

Betty's mouth dried. This could be the break

they'd been looking for. *I should have bugged the car.* "Did he ask you to put money in?"

Leonora shook her head. "Not yet. I think he was warming me up to the idea."

They had an opportunity to catch him in the act. A chance to get him on tape. Even though Alice had been against the idea, that had been primarily an objection to the garage's involvement, and at the last moment, Betty had thrown the bugging device into her suitcase. "I can bug your car with your consent. Later tonight."

She'd have to talk to Joe—let him in on at least part of the secret that she and Leonora were working together. Nerves danced in her stomach. *How will he take it?* The realization that she was more involved than he'd thought, was taking a considerably more active role than his overprotective nature would be happy with, might propel him to intervene. To try to make her back off. Every hour they'd spent together had brought them closer, had made them more in sync, but omissions were as bad as lies really. The arrangements had been made with Leonora before Joe's arrival on the scene, before she knew him. They couldn't move on to the next level, both in catching Charmers and in their relationship, without her coming clean.

Now they were partners—he needed to know.

"Give me your keys. I'll take care of it." *We'll take care of it.*

"Of course." Leonora opened her clutch bag and took out her car keys. "Slip the keys back to me tomorrow morning."

———

JOE COULDN'T TAKE his eyes off Betty as she and Leonora walked back to their table. She was a complete knockout in that dress, which cinched in her narrow waist and revealed a generous amount of cleavage. The material was sort of gathered in the front, and floated straight to the ground. He hadn't a clue about women's fashion, but whoever had created the dress knew how to showcase a woman's body all right.

He'd tried to get Charmers to open up while they were alone with no luck. The guy had spoken about the stock market, but he'd lost Joe when he's started talking about "dead cat bounce." He had to push harder, had to spark Charmers's interest.

"So the stock market is a no-no at the moment," he murmured. "Man, who would think coming into money would be such a headache? Leaving it in my account, earning peanuts…I just know there has to be a better way to go."

"I'll give it some thought," Charmers said, watching the women's approach. "Your navigator is very pretty. Have you been together long?"

There was something in his tone—admiration, but not directed at Betty, more directed at Joe.

Keeping his expression neutral, Joe responded. "Not very long, no. But she's very special to me."

"I can tell." There was a sly expression in Charmers's eyes. "You chose well."

Before Joe had a chance to tease out the hidden meaning behind Charmers's words, Leonora and Betty joined them at the table.

On stage, the rallymeister stood and introduced their auctioneer for the evening, and the auction began.

It appeared that all of the items in the auction had a local flavor. A few paintings by a prominent local artist came under the hammer first, followed by an all-expenses weekend at the hotel they were currently staying in. When the third lot was announced, Betty leaned forward, watching intently.

"A case of the award-winning Blue Heaven 2007 Vintage Red from our very own local Blue Vineyard," the auctioneer said.

She shot Joe a glance. "That was a very good year for them."

"This wine has won a gold medal, everyone, with a subtle blend of Bordeaux, merlot, cabernet sauvignon, and cabernet franc. Who'll give me $120 for the case?"

Betty held up one of the auction paddles they'd left on the table.

"We have $120 from the lady in red," the auctioneer said. "Who'll give me $150?"

The bidding raced upward. Betty continued to bid without batting an eyelid and was still in as the case reached $300. "That's about market price," she said to Joe.

"Do I hear $330?"

She gave up at $440 and by the time the final bid was cast, the case of wine had reached $1,600.

"I wonder what's up next." Her eyes were bright. "I love this, don't you?"

Joe had to bid on something, but what? A string of pearls from a local jeweler was next, more all-expenses-paid stays at various hotels in the vicinity, followed by a full service from Under the Hood garage. Then the auctioneer announced an item that stirred Joe's interest.

"We have a very special item next, ladies and gentlemen, donated by our very own Ed Fleming. Ed has donated his copy of the shooting script for the very first episode of *Crime Bite*." He held up the bound sheaf of paper. "Signed by Mr. Fleming and all the members of the cast, this is a priceless piece of memorabilia in the making, everyone, and remember, we're bidding for charity here. All the money raised here tonight will go to the Meadowsweet Women's Shelter. It's difficult to price this item—who'll give me $1,000?" Betty's smile widened as Joe lifted his paddle.

The room was obviously full of fans of the TV series. Bidding was fast and furious, and under normal circumstances Joe would have parked his paddle facedown on the table well before the bidding rose to $5,000. But this was no ordinary auction—he'd cleared expenditure with Bond earlier, so he kept on bidding until no one else wanted to play.

"$7,500 to the gentleman." The auctioneer looked straight at Joe. "Do I hear more?"

Joe glanced at Charmers, who raised his glass and nodded as if in admiration.

The room was silent.

"Sold." The auctioneer brought down his hammer.

Joe turned to Betty. "It's for you, baby."

Betty squealed, threw her arms around his neck, and kissed him like Christmas had come early. And this time, instead of holding back, of letting her dictate the pace, Joe pulled her close with one hand, found the nape of her neck with the other, and, room be damned, showed her he'd moved past pretending. The taste of her cracked open a fissure, revealing the molten heart of pure, unadulterated desire welling up inside him, demanding release.

When he eased away, the stunned expression in her eyes and the rapid rise and fall of her beautiful breasts told him more eloquently than words ever could that she felt the same.

He was done pretending that kissing her meant nothing.

# SEVEN

In the aftermath of *that kiss*, Betty struggled for objectivity. It was easy to understand why actors and actresses had affairs when they were on location. Pretending to love someone—staring into their eyes at every possible opportunity, kissing them, and acting out romance before an audience—was so heady it was difficult to separate fiction from reality.

If this evening had been real, rather than a show put on to fool a con man, it would have been one of the best of her life. Every time she looked at Joe, he was watching her with an intensity and appreciation that made her stomach clench.

He stroked her arm when they sat at the

table, lighting an internal fuse that sparked from his fingers through her entire body. He wasn't that good an actor. He was feeling it too.

Bidding had been fun, but when he'd started to bid for the *Crime Bite* script he'd turned to her and whispered, "For you," and her heart had just about melted.

There couldn't be anything sexier than a man focused on winning. His whole demeanor was relaxed but alert as he countered every bid with a smooth raise of his paddle. At some point in the proceedings she'd sneaked her hand under the table and laid it on his hard thigh.

His expression didn't alter, but a muscle jumped in the corner of his jaw.

If they really were a couple, he couldn't have given her a better gift if he'd tried. The purchase wouldn't happen—not on the FBI's paycheck—but maybe when this whole thing was over with she could buy the bid from them. She didn't like to flash her money around, but a souvenir of her favorite show would be worth it. And the profits were going to charity…

Leonora's news that Charmers had pitched the investment opportunity to her was huge. She had to tell Joe tonight, had to let him know everything that was going on…

"What are you thinking about?" Joe slipped a hand over hers.

"I've really enjoyed tonight." They were still at the table, but there was no pretense necessary. She had enjoyed it.

"I'm going to have to leave you lovebirds to it," Leonora said. She brought a hand to her forehead. "I have a terrible headache. I think I'll go and see if I can scare up some headache tablets from reception."

"I'll come with you," Charmers made to rise, but she stopped him with one hand to his arm.

"Don't let me spoil your evening, Alexander. I really need to lie down in a darkened room." She cast an apologetic glance at Charmers. "I want to be fresh for tomorrow."

Charmers nodded. "I'll walk you to your room, anyway." He turned to Joe and Betty. "See you at breakfast, then."

She waited until they had disappeared from view. "So, how did you get on? Did he bite?"

"I can't work him out at all. The guy is a closed book." Joe rubbed the side of his face. "A couple of times there he seemed to be warming up to me, but he's difficult to read."

The dining room was beginning to empty

out. Betty picked up her jeweled clutch. "Let's go."

---

JOE WALKED her to her door. He wished to hell things were different, and he could walk inside with her, act on the feelings that welled up within him every time she gave him that look. When she'd rested her hand on his thigh during the bidding he'd damned near swallowed his tongue. And that kiss—that kiss had changed everything. But he couldn't go inside with her. Had to stay focused. Couldn't let emotion cloud his objectivity.

"Come inside." She unlocked the door.

Heat had been spiraling through him all evening. And now she was so close her familiar scent filled him with every breath. This rally was supposed to be work, but he was having a hard time remembering that—he enjoyed her company too much. That red dress—he'd struggled to keep his hands off her. The smart thing was to say good-night at her door. To walk away. "I can't."

She pushed the door open and tugged his hand. "You have to."

With a sigh, he gave in to the inevitable and followed her inside. She was impossible to resist —she knew more of his secrets than most, and seemed okay with them. Maybe when this was all over they could have something. He reached for her but she stepped away.

She flicked on the light, kicked off her shoes, and walked to the bed. "Come on over here." She sat down, scooted up the bed, propped up the pillow as a support for her back, and crossed her legs. "I'm not trying to seduce you, we need to talk."

*Okay, that's unexpected.* He sauntered over and joined her. "What's up?"

"I haven't been one hundred percent honest." Her face scrunched up and she picked at the fabric of her gown.

"I don't like the sound of this…"

"I'm just going to say it." She took a deep breath. Raised her eyes to his. "When I first saw Charmers with Leonora—well, I told her."

Ice trickled down Joe's spine. "Told her what, exactly?"

"I told her he was a rotten, lying scumbag. And that he was trying to con her. Leonora and I have been working together."

*Jesus.* "When the…why the hell didn't you tell me this before?"

"And while I'm at it, I guess I should tell you that Alice knows all about it too."

His world shifted. All his preconceived notions about what they were doing, what their mission was, fractured. He'd thought he was in control, he was running this operation, but now…Joe felt sucker punched, light-headed at the information coming at him. "Do they both know I'm FBI?"

She nodded.

"And Mark?"

"No. We didn't tell Mark. No one else knows. I didn't tell you sooner because I didn't know you, I wasn't sure…"

*She didn't trust him.* All the time he'd been opening up, sharing his inner thoughts and memories of making invisible ink with his mother, thinking about baring his goddamned soul, she'd been keeping secrets. Hiding facts. He clenched his teeth together.

For a moment there he'd let himself believe this was going somewhere, had let his body's reaction to her guide his heart. He sucked in a breath, stood, and paced across the room and back. *Think of the mission.* This changed everything. If they had set this whole thing up, Charmers could claim that it was an attempt at entrapment. He could walk on a technicality. "Tell me about how this started."

"I saw them together at the farmers' market. He'd already met Leonora and started to make some moves on her. I couldn't stand to see the same thing that happened to my mother happen to her, so I told her everything. Leonora wanted to help."

"You could have endangered her, making her go through with this—neither of you are professionals…" Having Betty involved had been a far-from-ideal situation, but the addition of Leonora and Alice as well was catastrophic. The more people involved, the greater the possibility of failure.

"I didn't make Leonora go through with anything. I just told her what sort of man he was." Her eyes flashed. "And yes, we're not professionals. But professionals haven't been exactly brilliant at catching him either." She crossed her arms. "Anyway, I'm telling you now." Her face scrunched up. "I didn't want to put my trust in the authorities after what happened before, but I've thought long and hard about this and I've decided I have to. I know you want the same thing I do. This evening, Leonora told me things have escalated. Today he mentioned an investment opportunity to her, and I think we should bug their car." She got up from the bed, and rooted around in her luggage. "I bought this."

Joe took the tiny recording device from her outstretched hand. He recognized the unit; it was not up to FBI standard, but probably one of the best amateur devices out there. He'd planned to bug the car himself before the rally began, but they hadn't been able to get a warrant in time. Leonora's involvement changed that—with her consent there was no impediment to placing the recording device there.

"Where did you get this?"

She grinned, and the part of himself that wanted her took another hit.

"There's a store in Chesapeake that carries a range of surveillance equipment and other supplies. I bought a few things I thought I might need once I identified Charmers."

His memory stirred. "Like the fingerprinting kit."

She nodded. "I bought a Tyvek suit, booties, and gloves too, in case I got an opportunity to search his house."

The thought of her breaking and entering… "You didn't, though, did you?"

"No. I haven't had a chance yet. I bought a lock-picking kit and have watched a lot of videos on YouTube to prepare, though—I've gotten pretty good at it." That smile again, the one that curled past his defenses and squeezed his heart.

She couldn't try anything foolish. All of his protective instincts made his voice harsh. "You mustn't put yourself in danger. I'm here now. We're a team."

"Okay." She meant it. "Leonora gave me her car key this evening. I thought we could just wait until everyone is asleep and then sneak out and plant it."

Usually when an agent's cover was so comprehensively blown, there was no other alternative but to walk away. But he couldn't. He examined the listening device. All of her amateur sleuthing had been worth it—this listening device might be the very thing to gather the evidence they needed. "You did good," he admitted.

He slipped the device into his pocket. "I'll deal with this from here on in. Give me her car keys."

"I can…"

"No. I'll do it." She'd done enough already; it was time to reestablish control over this situation. Do the job he was being paid to do. He glanced at his watch. "I need to talk to Leonora before morning."

Betty rooted in her clutch, pulled out the keys, and handed them over, then took out her cell phone. "I'll call her—she'll be expecting my call anyway. We've been in contact every night." She rang, and quickly filled Leonora in on the situation. Her eyes were bright, and her shoulders were tense. She couldn't stop fiddling with the draped shoulder of her dress, and moving back and forth, so buzzing with electricity she practically sparked. Eventually, she handed the phone over.

"Leonora."

"I'm so glad you're in on our secret, Joe," Leonora said.

"Me too." He shot a glance at Betty, then walked across the room and pulled aside the curtain to stare out into the black night sky. "With your permission, we're going to bug the car tonight, but it's imperative that you don't lead him in conversation tomorrow. You have to let him suggest the investment opportunity to you—you can't be the one to bring it up. Do you understand?"

"He should say it. Yes."

"If you mention it first, it could be considered entrapment. If that happens, he will walk." His voice sounded harsh to his own ears, but there was nothing he could do about that. She had to understand—couldn't screw this up.

"I get it."

"Okay." He let the curtain drop, and walked back to hand the phone over to Betty. He held up the recording device. "I'll take care of this later. I'll give you the keys in the morning." He was a damn good agent, as long as he kept his head in the game, but had been too close to being distracted by a make-believe relationship taking form. Her revelations tonight had come just at the right time, had doused him in a cold splash of reality. Getting involved with someone who didn't trust him was a crazy mistake he shouldn't make.

Joe turned away from her and walked out of the door.

*WHAT JUST HAPPENED?* Betty said good-night to Leonora and stared at the door. She'd expected that he'd be pissed, but this…obviously Joe wasn't the sort of man to talk it out. Instead, the moment he'd gotten over his shock at her news he'd shut down completely.

Shut down and walked out.

The understanding that had been growing between them, the warm feeling of being partners in this, had been cut dead with the tightening of his jaw. He'd taken the keys and recording device and walked out as though there was nothing more to say—nothing more to do. She got up and stripped off her dress. Didn't bother to put on her pajamas, just crawled into bed and stared at the ceiling.

He'd acted just like he had on the first day they met. Had rewound their relationship back to the beginning, was trying to make them strangers again. This wasn't going to work. There was more to life than catching Charmers. There was fun, friendship, love.

He might very well be able to turn off his emotions, but she couldn't. *Wouldn't.*

"Dammit!" If she'd waited a few minutes to tell him—if she'd gone with her gut and moved toward rather than away from his hand that first moment in her room, maybe things would have turned out differently. Maybe he'd be joining her in bed, rather than freezing her out.

"Crap, crap, crap!" She kicked off the duvet and dragged on a pair of jeans and a black T-shirt. Slipped her feet into her Converse. There was no way she could sleep now, not with this eating away at her.

# EIGHT

There was a quick rap at his door. Joe was in the process of getting changed. He'd stripped off his shirt and shed his shoes and socks, so he walked to the door barefoot.

The moment he cracked the door open, it pushed inward, propelled by a very determined female hand.

Betty stormed in, eyes flashing. "You can't just walk out like that." She planted her hands on her hips. "I know you're angry, but..." Her gaze flickered down to his naked chest and her lips parted a fraction. "Um..."

"What more is there to say? I know about Leonora's involvement—I'm taking care of things. You should get some sleep, tomorrow is—"

"Screw tomorrow." She stepped as close as a person could get without actually colliding. Placed a hand on his chest. "Dammit, Joe. You and me are more than this case. I want—" She looked at his mouth.

He knew what she wanted. He wanted it too. "You're the most infuriating woman in the world." He couldn't stop himself, even if his life depended on it. One hand went to the side of her face while the other slipped around her waist, jerking her body to his. Then he kissed her, hard, hot, and hungry.

She tasted of strawberries. Softened in his arms and seemed to melt against his chest. By coming into his room, she'd tested his resolve to stay away from her at a moment when he was too vulnerable, wanted her too strongly to have a hope of resisting. He grabbed the hem of her black T-shirt and pulled it off in one smooth movement, loving the way her arms immediately fastened around his neck the moment she was stripped of it. She wasn't wearing a bra, and the feel of her warmth against him heated his blood. With labored breaths he stroked his fingers down her spine, breathed in her distinctive scent, and tasted the soft skin of her neck.

"You've bewitched me."

Her mouth curved in a smile. "Good."

He claimed her mouth again, and took her to bed.

IT WAS a moment out of time. In a room comfortably sterile, luxuriously neutral. The sexual pull between them was so strong, she'd been attracted like an iron filing to a powerful magnet. Their being together was as inevitable as the sun's climb into the sky every morning.

Betty was no stranger to physical intimacy. She'd had a pleasant fling for a couple of months with the bartending owner of their local haunt, Mike's. Her business partners didn't understand. Before meeting Heath, Mel had some weird hang-ups about sex, and Alice was such a romantic, she couldn't wrap her head around casual.

Mike had been an accomplished lover, she couldn't fault his technique.

But this—this was different. At the mere touch of Joe's lips on her neck, her temperature soared. When he palmed her breast, goosebumps appear on her skin. His touch sent a magical tingle through her veins, like electricity travelling along wires to every inch of her body.

Joe stripped off the remainder of his clothes, and helped Betty out of hers.

"You're very beautiful." His voice was a deep murmur that made the hair on the back of her neck stand up straight. His fingers skimmed her ribcage. He flipped over on the king-sized bed and she curved against his side. "This isn't—"

"Shhh and kiss me." She knew what he was about to say. That this wasn't supposed to happen. They were on assignment. An important undercover mission that had to succeed. In order to maintain their cover, they were supposed to look like a couple in love, who were sleeping together. But that it was an illusion. Having sex wasn't part of the plan. Might complicate everything.

Betty knew the reasons why this was a bad idea.

She just chose to disregard them.

Joe's lips were firm and warm. His tongue teased the seam of her mouth, before they started to kiss as though it was the first time either of them had ever kissed anyone like this before.

Betty was melting. Everything was Joe. The woodsy scent of him, a faint hint of the aftershave he used. Every point they made contact was energized and super sensitized. She could kiss him forever. *We don't have forever.*

She pushed away the thought. Smoothed her hands over his chest. His heart was beating fast under her fingertips. She wanted to be nearer. Needed more of his heat.

His hands curved around her ribcage, and effortlessly, he lifted her on top of him.

Compelled by desire, she opened her legs and settled her core on top of his hard length. Shifted against him, feeling him against her so arousing she couldn't hold back an impassioned groan.

"Wait." Joe moved her down a fraction, to his thighs. "Condom." He reached off the bed, retrieved his wallet from the bedside table and found a small foil packet.

He quickly sheathed himself, then angled himself up to reach her again. Open mouthed kisses. Hands playing with her sensitive nipples, then curving around her to press her breasts into his chest.

Joe shifted so he was sitting up in bed with his back against the hard wooden headboard.

Betty sat on his lap, shivering at the sensation of his hardness rubbing against her sensitive core. Her back arched.

"Let me taste you."

She was holding on to the last sliver of control as it was. If Joe put his mouth on her, she would lose it for sure, and she knew what she wanted. What she needed.

Betty shook her head.

Joe's mouth curved in a sensual smile. "No?" He kissed the spot where her neck met her shoulder. The soft brush of his hair against her skin, delicious.

"I want something else." She'd never been shy before, but something about this encounter had pierced her usual composure. Everything about making love with Joe was so much more than it had been with anyone else. This compelling desperate feeling within her was more than want, it was need. A clawing need for physical release she'd never felt with anyone before.

Joe's thumb stroked her jawline. He tilted her head a fraction, so she had no option but to look at him. Could he see the vulnerability in her eyes? How shaky and out of control she felt, here in his arms?

"Tell me." He didn't look away. Didn't put any pressure on her, just waited patiently, open and caring.

"I want you inside me," Betty whispered. "I need you inside me right now."

He looked at her lips. Kissed her so softly, something inside broke open. Then he grasped her hips, helped her rise off him a fraction, and positioned himself at her entrance.

When he thrust into her the first time, she sighed. The second, she groaned. After that, everything melded together into a sensual celebration of touching and tasting, loving and giving. She'd lost herself. He had too. It was evident in the muttered endearments he spoke into her ear, into her tousled hair. They moved as one, both chasing the ultimate release.

There was no time to be self-conscious. No need for anything but the basic honesty of their need, their desperate need.

When the rhythm of their bodies switched to frantic, they clung to each other as though tomorrow might never come. Betty's teeth grazed Joe's neck. His earlobe.

The intensity of the moment was so strong

she probably screamed when she came. If not, she did in her mind.

And when the spasms of her orgasm faded and Joe held her tightly in his arms as if he never wanted to let her go, she refused to listen to the insistent little voice of reason in her head that told her to face the truth. And let herself pretend.

WHEN BETTY WOKE the following morning the bed next to her was empty. She touched the space he'd lain in and found it cold. There was no sound from the bathroom. The clothes he'd worn the previous night hung in the wardrobe, and hers had been picked up off the floor, carefully folded, and placed on a chair next to the bed, with Leonora's keys placed on top.

She scooted up in the bed, holding the sheet to cover her chest. Called his name softly, just in case, but there was no reply. A pale, watery light bled in from the crack in the drapes—it must still be early. The empty room and rapidly cooling bed held no appeal. She dressed quickly, shoved the keys into her pocket, and went back to her room.

Thoughts of the night before replayed in her mind as she stood under a shower hot enough to create a fog in the room. She breathed in the steam and let the water stream over her head, over her closed eyes. She'd been so angry the night before. So determined to make him acknowledge her, acknowledge them, she hadn't thought through the consequences of her actions.

The moment his control snapped and he'd kissed her so masterfully, reason had evaporated. They'd both been swirled up in a maelstrom of passion, unable to think, unable to do anything but feel. The times she'd been in his arms before were pale shadows compared to really being with him—of meaning every single touch. They hadn't spoken from the moment they climbed into bed together, apart from softly murmured words that made little sense. Appreciation of each other's bodies. Sighs and shared laughter.

Being with him had been wonderful.

They'd been as close as two people possibly could be, alone in an intimate bubble, safe from the world outside. Now it was over, and who knew what today would hold?

JOE'S LEG muscles burned as he slowed from a
run to a walk on approaching the hotel. When
he'd woken, Betty was curled around him from
behind, her hand lay on his stomach, and her
steady breaths tickled his back with every exhale.
He'd edged away, and spent long moments
watching her. Her long eyelashes dusted against
her pale skin. Her hair curled against her cheek
and spread across his pillow. Her lips were pink.
Their remembered softness drew him. His hand
hovered over her bare shoulder before he pulled
it back, closed his eyes, and swallowed. It had
taken everything he had to climb out of bed,
dress, and go outside.

In the past, running had been a cure for
most of his ills. Once his muscles started to
pound the grass, and his breath evened out, he
usually lost himself in the rhythm, pushed out
thought, and let his mind roam free. Not this
time.

Every step was a step away from her. He'd
even tried to think of Charmers, to turn his
mind on to the matter at hand, the task he had
to do. But where once that would have been
enough to consume him, it was no longer. He
hadn't been lying when he'd told her she'd
bewitched him—she'd moved into his head and

taken permanent residence. Even the ache of her deception was impossible to reclaim.

He'd run for an hour. Had pushed his body to its limits in the cool morning air. And still, clear, concise thought was beyond him.

Joe rubbed a hand over the back of his neck as he quietly opened the door to his room. She wasn't there. A check of the bathroom revealed no sign. He breathed in deep, catching a trace of her in the air. Then went to shower.

It was almost nine when he tapped on her door. There was no answer, so he went downstairs. Breakfast was being served in a glass-walled conservatory with a stunning view of the violet mountains.

She sat alone at a table, with a large French press of coffee and a huge breakfast before her.

"Hi."

She looked up and smiled. "I wondered where you'd gotten to." There was no censure in her tone, no edge to her words. Her smile was genuine. "This breakfast is to die for."

"It looks like it might kill you by clogging up your arteries."

She picked up a piece of crispy bacon and bit it. "Feel free to order the oatmeal then. Me? I'm all for dying happy."

He pulled out a chair. She tapped the side of her face. "What, no kiss?"

Obediently, he leaned over and brought his lips to her cheek. "I got the keys back to Leonora," she whispered. "They're over there... don't look."

So the kiss was for show. He sat and picked up the menu, shaking off a totally crazy sensation of disappointment that they seemed to be back at square one. Further on in the investigation, but acting as though the night before, the night that he'd thought would change things, had never happened.

SHE WOULDN'T HAVE PEGGED him as a granola man. As Joe ate, Betty mentally patted herself on the back for managing to keep it together.

"I went for an early-morning run," Joe said.

She wasn't surprised—a body like his didn't just happen; it made sense that he worked at it. "I just went with the early-morning snooze. So I guess we're all set for today. For, you know..." She shifted her glance to Charmers without moving her head.

"Yeah, we're all set." He grinned. "You definitely watch too many cop shows."

"Are you saying I'm not subtle?" Warmth spread through her at the look in his eyes. The same look that had been in them in the quiet of the night. An intimate, private look that effectively made the rest of the room recede. For a long moment, she just lived. Just breathed. Didn't question or run potential future scenarios as she had been all morning. Just let it be.

"Your eggs are getting cold."

She pushed her plate away. "I couldn't eat another bite."

Around them, the room was beginning to thin out. Joe finished his breakfast and drained his coffee cup. "I guess it's time to go."

Plotting the course from the new route book onto the map was much easier the second time around. The first time she'd done it, she'd been fretting about how much time she had to do it, but confidence swelled inside as she deftly marked the map.

As yesterday, Joe stood to one side with the other drivers as the navigators worked on this essential first element of their journeys. Leonora was on the other side of the table, doing the same thing. They'd met in the restroom this morning for the key return, and Leonora was much calmer today with the knowledge that Joe was on board. That it wasn't just the two of them.

Truth be told, she was glad to have him by her side too. Admitting that she'd been a little overwhelmed was against her nature, but now that someone had both her and Leonora's backs…well, it was reassuring.

"Five minutes," the rallymeister said.

She checked her calculations, picked up their time card, and stowed her pens, then they were off.

Everything seemed easier as they sped from the hotel on the day's first stage. "Okay, back the way we came, then we're taking a left a mile ahead." She peered out of the windshield. "And you're gunning it again, Speedy. Slow down a little."

"Understood, ma'am." His voice was deep and delicious.

"I like you calling me ma'am."

He shot her a glance. "Oh yeah?"

"Mmm. It's sort of like you're a Marine or something."

He raised an eyebrow. "Have you got a thing for men in uniform? Because all I have for work is a black suit, which doesn't quite cut it, but I'm sure I could…"

"Dress up?" She felt slightly faint at the thought of it.

"Sure." The corner of his mouth twitched. "So what's your fantasy? Soldier, sailor, doctor?"

*Doesn't matter, as long as the uniform has you in it.* "That turn is coming up." She consulted the map and pointed ahead. "Next left."

They worked together like a well-oiled engine. Timing the route was tricky, requiring her attention, but every time she managed to grab a chance to look at him he seemed happy. Not exactly smiling—his smiles had to be earned —but more than content. He drove with a sure-handed skill reminiscent of the way he'd held her the night before.

Her mouth dried as her memories blossomed, crowding out the task at hand. The feel of his hard chest under her questing fingers. The sounds he made as she bit his neck gently…

"Earth to Betty. You still with me, ma'am?"

She pressed her lips together. Blinked a couple of times. "Yup." Her eyes focused on the page again.

"You said five miles, and we've almost done that. What's next?"

She ticked off a couple of steps on the route map that she'd ignored while in her biting-Joe haze. "Okay, the road should start to wind to the right, then left, and then we should be coming up on a control point." She checked their time. "Two seconds behind. Speed up a little."

"Speed up—slow down—you're never satisfied."

"I wouldn't say that."

Joe actually laughed.

They hit the control point with no penalties, and followed the route as it cut though a thick swath of forest. Bitter-chocolate tree trunks and pine needles in shades of oriental jade cut into the edges of the road, creating a living tunnel.

"I love the mountains." Betty opened the window a crack and sniffed the air. "When you're not undercover, where do you live?"

His jaw tightened a notch. His hands gripped the steering wheel more tightly as he stared out the windshield. "I have an apartment in Chicago. I guess I'm based there." His voice was terse. The shift in mood subtle, but unmistakable—as if sharing personal details of his real life was not part of the deal.

She continued on, regardless. "Does your family live there?"

"I don't have family." He glanced over. "I could do with something to drink. Could you pass me a bottle of water?"

He took the bottle she handed over and drank.

Her previous enjoyment of their surroundings paled. *Okay, he doesn't want to talk about family.* The physical intimacy they'd shared the night before didn't seem to extend to an emotional one. But it was early days in their relationship; maybe over time he'd open up and share more. She took a bottle of water from the cooler for herself and concentrated on feeding him further directions from the route map for the next hour.

"I wish we could hear what's going on in Leonora's car. I really want him to have mentioned the investment opportunity again. If he does, if he asks her to give him money to invest, is that enough to get him?" It would be so great to have this whole thing over with. To get back to ordinary life. Maybe to see if they could exist as a couple outside the hothouse of the investigation.

"No. We need him to actually take her money and either run or lodge it in one of his accounts. So far, he's followed a predictable pattern. He gets a check, moves it into his Carlisle account, and…"

"Goes on a business trip. In my mother's case, anyway." She screwed up her face at the memory. "She didn't even suspect him until he'd been gone for over a week. He kept in telephone contact for a few days, then his cell mysteriously stopped working. The private investigator said it was a throwaway."

"Fits the pattern."

Betty ticked off another section of the route book. "We continue down here for ten miles, then we're stopping for lunch. I think we've got a real chance of winning the leaders' jerseys tonight." If only figuring out the future of their relationship was as simple.

# NINE

Betty was desperate for a break when they arrived at the lunch spot. They'd timed their arrival almost perfectly, scoring only a couple of penalties for the last stage. Her legs were stiff and her ass was numb after the hours in the car.

The organizers had outdone themselves this time. They'd received permission to host the lunch at a large private house with beautiful gardens. The weather was crisp, but clear and bright. Perfect.

The cars parked on a gravel sweep outside the house, and a couple of restrooms had been made available. Betty climbed out of the MG, stretched up, bent to touch her toes, then shook out her legs. Charmers exited Leonora's Rolls and strode off.

"I'll go talk to Leonora."

Joe nodded. "People are walking around the side of the house; I think lunch is in the garden. I'll grab us a couple of seats."

Leonora looked up from stowing her map when Betty tapped on the window, and jerked her head indicating Betty should slip into the driver's seat.

Betty had barely closed the door when Leonora started speaking. "I got it. He asked me to invest." She pulled in her bottom lip and worried it with her teeth. "He wants me to organize it tomorrow afternoon—when we come back from the rally. He says the investment is time-sensitive and he wants to get our money in before Monday."

"How much?"

"Twenty thousand." Leonora's eyebrows pulled together in a frown. "Are you sure we should risk it? Twenty thousand is a lot of money."

Not wanting their absence to be noticed, Betty quickly reassured Leonora and talked through the internet banking procedure. It was so important to ensure that the evidence remained untainted, she couldn't help but check again. "You didn't lead him in any way…"

Leonora shook her head. "No. It was perfect. He just brought it up while he was driving. The recording will prove that."

They had him.

The end was so close she could taste it.

Elation bubbled through Betty's veins as she hurried from the car to find Joe. A huge glass conservatory was attached to the back of the house. The garden was full of colorful flowers, but they faded into insignificance when she turned the corner and took in the whole view.

A sparkling cascade fell from an exposed cliff overhanging the end of the garden. The sheet of glistening whitewater foamed into a pool of green water, around which were large circular tables set with silverware and crystal.

She stopped, the ache in her legs instantly forgotten. Breathed in the scented air and let the tension of the morning flow from her with the exhale. *What was it about waterfalls that made them so magical?*

"It's beautiful, isn't it?" Charmers walked up beside her. "The rallymeister owns a beautiful property."

"He owns this?"

Charmers took her arm. "He has the best of everything. Shall we join the others?"

Charmers's touch was repulsive; she had to force herself not to stiffen, not to pluck his hand off her like a caterpillar on a rose. To the casual observer he was a distinguished and pleasant man, good-looking, wealthy, and well-spoken. The type of guy who pulled chairs out for women.

But looks could be deceiving, and despite appearances, he was the type of guy who pulled chairs out from under women.

"You and Joe make a lovely couple." Even his voice made the hairs on the back of her neck rise.

"Thank you." Could he see the insincerity of her smile? She bared more of her top teeth, forced the curve of her lips upward until her cheeks ached.

At last, he released her.

"Isn't this place amazing?" She pulled up a chair and sank down in it, panic subsiding being close to Joe again. "That waterfall is so beautiful."

"When we've eaten we'll have to walk over and check it out." His eyes were sending her messages, ones she couldn't answer at the table.

She picked up a white linen napkin, shook it out, and laid it over her lap, then gazed across the lawn to the conservatory, where an army of servers were making their way to the tables, laden with dishes of food. "Looking forward to it."

HE'D HATED SEEING Charmers's hand on her. As they walked across the grass, Joe's hands had curled into fists below the table. His face ached with the effort of keeping his expression neutral. Betty's back was straight; her smile was fixed. No one there would be aware of just how she was feeling, but he knew—she hated it just as much as he did.

When Charmers had glanced over at Joe, then spoken to her, her smile was wide. It would fool anyone who didn't know her, and probably most of those who did. But it didn't fool Joe.

The meal was great, but it may as well have been cardboard. While Leonora and Betty had been inside, he'd made a quick call to Bond and gained some important intel and he needed to talk to Betty about it. He also wanted to know what exactly Leonora had told Betty, as soon as possible. They didn't linger over coffee, but made their excuses to the table and, holding hands, walked over to the waterfall.

"What did Leonora say?"

For appearances, Joe rubbed her arm. Pulled her close. The wall of water glistened in the sunlight, and a diffused mist of water cooled the air.

"He asked Leonora to invest." She turned in his arms and rested her head against his chest. To anyone looking on it must look like a tender moment. "He wants her to transfer the money into his account tomorrow, when we get back to Meadowsweet."

"He said all this in the car?" A subtle perfume rose from her hair—it could only be the same hotel shampoo he'd used, but on her, added in with her own unique scent, it was fresh and intoxicating. Her body was warm against him. Kissing her here would crystallize a memory he'd have forever. He swallowed. Forced his mind back to the job. "She didn't…"

"He spoke; she agreed. Just as we'd planned." She looked up. Her lips parted.

Joe leaned in, brushed his lips against hers, and then eased away. "Let's walk."

She linked her arm through his as they

walked around the waterfall.

"I have news too. I spoke to Bond. The woman he conned after your mother was also in the Hamptons. She didn't report it either, but they've talked to her and she knows your mother. Her name is Helen Dawkins. Do you know her?"

Betty frowned. "No. But my mother has many friends I don't know. Before Charmers, I was very caught up in my own life. I didn't spend enough time with her." She rubbed the back of her neck. "I neglected her, I guess."

"Dawkins will testify. But when she does, your mother's name will be out in the open as the woman who introduced her to Charmers. I know your mother doesn't want to testify, but…"

Betty grimaced. "I just don't want to put her through it. If I'd come home when she asked, if I'd checked him out, maybe this wouldn't have happened to her."

Guilt was driving her. Putting up roadblocks and making her determined to protect her mother from public scrutiny. Shame that she hadn't been there to save her mother from getting involved with Charmers.

The same guilt that drove him for allowing Charmers to continue conning woman after woman since he'd weaseled out of custody. Joe stopped and faced the tumbling water. She wouldn't like what he had to say, but he had no choice. He had to come clean. He breathed deep.

"It wasn't your fault. You know Charmers has done this before—more than once. The FBI almost had him…"

"But he walked. I know."

The need to justify his actions, to make her understand, burned in Joe's chest. "You don't know everything. I've been tracking Charmers for years. I'm the one who messed up. I wanted him so bad I took my eye off a key piece of evidence, contaminated the chain of custody." He couldn't bear to look at her. Couldn't bear to see the condemnation that must be in her eyes. "I couldn't have saved your mother, but I could have saved some of them. Should have saved them."

Silence stretched for a long moment, then finally she spoke. "Joe."

He turned.

"After he walked"—she swallowed—"the case was over, wasn't it?"

"Not for me. I kept monitoring accounts that he might have been associated with."

"Against your boss's orders?"

"He didn't exactly know about it until I got a lead when Charmers used plastic in Meadowsweet."

His determination had brought him head-to-head with his boss on more than one occasion. Bond had been adamant that the case was over. Had said he was focused to the point of obsession on getting Charmers and that his objectivity was skewed as a result. Bond had given the order to stop looking, but that was an order Joe couldn't accept. He shouldn't have even been still monitoring people of interest to the case, shouldn't have been alerted when Corben's account had shown a withdrawal after such a long time. But he'd been sure one day the con man would reappear. Had refused to let it go. His determination to reopen the case and find another way to bring Charmers to justice had brought them here. Had given him the chance to work with Betty, to be with her.

He guessed he had something to thank Charmers for.

"So your boss wanted you to let it go."

"He wanted me to, yeah."

"But you didn't." There was understanding in her eyes. "You couldn't let it go any more than I can. You screwed up, but you're brave enough to keep on trying to right that mistake." She squeezed his arm. "I'm not going to lie. It's difficult for me to hear that you're the agent I've spent years blaming for everything—but mistakes happen. And it's how you deal with the aftermath that counts."

Her forgiveness and understanding was a prize he didn't deserve, but gratefully accepted anyway. He turned to face her, pulled her close, felt her soft breasts press against his chest.

"Thank you." He breathed in the lemony scent of her hair. "I know we seem to have him, but I need to double-and triple-check every single element I can. I have to try to make sure that if one element collapses, we have more to fall back on. That there is no possibility of him getting away again. I need to talk to your mother."

"Okay." She kissed his cheek. "Let's do it now." They had time before the race started again, so they went back to the MG to make the call. Betty explained the situation to her mother, then handed the phone over.

"Mrs. Tremaine, Joe Carter, FBI. I understand you've already spoken to Agent Bond about your friend Helen Dawkins?"

A swift intake of breath. "Yes. She lives a

couple of miles away. We move in the same circles, but we're not close…I feel terrible that he met her through me. I warned everyone off him, but I should have given my friends details, I should have told them he was a criminal." Her voice shook.

"Miss Dawkins has agreed to testify against him. You said to Agent Bond that you weren't sure about that? That you needed to talk to your daughter before making that decision?"

Betty frowned.

"Yes, it's all such a shock, I need to talk to Betty, she—"

"I don't mean to pressure you, ma'am, but we need your decision on this as soon as possible. When Miss Dawkins testifies, your name will be in the public domain, and there won't be any escaping the fact that he met her through you. A lot of women have been taken in by him, but you are the first one we've found—you're the first link on this chain."

Christine Tremaine's gasp was audible. "You mean if I'd reported him this entire crime spree might have been caught in the bud? Everyone else might have…" She started to sob quietly.

"Now, ma'am, there's no need to get upset—"

Betty took the phone from his hand. "Mom, calm down. Charmers is a really slippery fish. Even the FBI let him go when they caught him later, remember? Don't worry about this now. I'll call you tonight." She held the phone away and disconnected the call. "She feels bad enough already—you didn't need to pile on the guilt."

Joe ground his back teeth together. "We're running out of time."

"You've got one witness, and after I've spoken to my mother you'll probably have two." She glared at him. "But people come before work, Joe. People are more important. Have a little sensitivity."

---

SHE READ directions off the route book—ticked them off as he completed them. Kept communication to a minimum as she tried to wrap her mind around everything that had happened. Her mother's confidence had been badly shaken by the con. Nowadays, she didn't do anything without careful consideration and discussion beforehand. It looked like there would be no chance of keeping her mother's name out of the papers, and she'd probably have to testify.

But she needed to be reassured in making that decision.

"What did Charmers say to you?" Joe asked.

"He was saying what a good couple we made." She thought so too. After last night, the thought of a future with him had flickered through her mind like a crazy dream. The sex was great and they'd had fun together. But they were very different people—lived in different places.

"He's right. We do make a good couple."

She shot him a glance. "So what happens after?" *What happens to us, when this case is over?*

"Once the deposit is made into his account?" Joe continued speaking without waiting for her answer. "I'll be on the first flight out to Chicago. There will be a lot of paperwork to do, and a lot of loose ends to tie up. Catching him is just the first step. The case won't be over until I've nailed down all the evidence—have brought him before a judge."

The case. Everything was all about the case. She'd let herself believe there might be a future for them, but his single-minded pursuit of Charmers didn't seem to take her, or them, into account. She stared out the window, blinking away threatening tears as the scenery sped past.

"I'm sorry if you thought I was insensitive to your mother—I understand how protective you are of her. I was the same about my mother too."

*Was?* He'd taken a brick out of his emotional wall to give her a glimpse through. "Is your mother…dead?"

He nodded. "She died a few years ago. She was my family. My father still lives, but we both gave up on him a long time ago." His mouth twisted. "Things are moving fast with you and me—I never planned that we'd become involved, but we have. Right now the goal is to get Charmers. I can't take my eye off that for a moment." He glanced over. "But when this is over, I don't want it to be the end for us."

Emotion welled up inside at his words. "I don't either." Needing physical contact with him, she rested a hand on his arm.

"I care about you, Betty." His voice was gruff. "Let's discuss this later."

"Okay."

He was right. The goal must be to bring Charmers to justice—by whatever means. Until that was done everything else would have to take second place. She consulted the map. "Three miles, then take a left."

An hour later they cleared the next time control point. She handed over a bottle of water to Joe, then her cell rang in her bag.

She pulled it out and glanced at the picture on the screen. "It's Alice."

"Hey."

"How's the race going?" Alice asked. "Are you winning?"

"Well, we're still in it." She hadn't expected to hear from her partner while they were on the rally; reception in the mountains could be spotty. "What's up?"

"I know you're busy— but I wanted to give you a heads-up. There's been a development. Leonora's son is here."

"He's not supposed to be back for a couple of weeks…"

"Well he's definitely here. He got home early. He doesn't want his mother to know—his deployment is over and he wants to surprise her at the Hunter's Moon Festival. The entire town is buzzing with the news. I thought you and Joe should know."

The turn was coming up. Betty covered the phone and passed on directions to Joe.

"Where is he staying? Is he at Leonora's house?"

"No. He's in the hotel here in town. The rally organizers have planned to bring him out after they announce the winners of the race tomorrow night before the festival. The whole town has been sworn to secrecy."

"Okay, I'll tell him. Talk to you later." She disconnected the call and shoved her cell back in her bag. "We may have a problem. Josh De Witt, Leonora's son, finished his deployment early and is waiting to surprise Leonora in Meadowsweet."

Joe's eyebrows pulled together. "Crap. That could be a major problem. Charmers's MO is to run before a member of the family shows up."

So even if she'd made it back to Christine, he could have cut and run, knowing she was on her way? "He's hiding out at the hotel. It can still work. If Leonora gives him the money in the afternoon, Charmers won't know Josh is even in the country until the evening."

"The minute Charmers finds out, he'll run. Coming face-to-face with a mark's son is not something he'll want to do. Especially once he has Leonora's money."

Betty cracked open a bottle of water and sipped to moisten her dry mouth. "When the rally is over we'll only have hours."

A flurry of activity lay ahead, after which Joe

would leave for Chicago. Would there be time to talk about their future before he left? Did he really even want to discuss it, or was he just keeping her pacified so as not to jeopardize the assignment?

---

THEY ACHIEVED AN ALMOST perfect score on their time card on returning to the hotel, but there was no time to celebrate.

"I need to talk to my people," Joe said as they walked to their rooms.

"I've got stuff to do too." Relaxing in the tub was pretty high on her list of priorities. "I should call Alice back," she said more to herself than to Joe, who had his key in the lock and his back turned to her.

"Don't go down to dinner without me." He squeezed her hand, but didn't kiss her. "I'll come get you."

"Okay." What point could there be to talk to Alice now? Her friend would be dying to know the details of the past couple of days—would no doubt be digging for romantic details. She opened her door, slipped in, and closed it. Rested her back against the cool wood and closed her eyes. Tonight she could sleep alone, or spend another night wrapped around Joe. Her body voted for the second option, but her head urged caution.

His words in the car had been heartfelt, but how realistic would persuing a relationship be, once his time in Meadowsweet was over? She'd thought she could just have fun, but something had changed along the way—her heart had gotten involved. He wasn't a man she could easily walk away from when this was over. Somehow the strands that pulled them together had become tangled and knotted. If she were smart, she'd put the brakes on now, save herself from heartbreak, but she wasn't smart. And she couldn't deny herself what might be their last night together.

She did what she had to do, then dressed for dinner in the other designer gown she'd packed, the gold Azzedine Alaïa. The strapless style clung to her curves, and the ruche flattered. Every time she wore it her confidence soared. She slipped her feet into nude heels, and fastened a large statement necklace around her neck. Nothing else was needed—she left her hair loose around her shoulders and added subtle makeup.

She transferred her wallet into her clutch bag and picked up her phone.

There was a knock at the door.

Every man looks great in a tuxedo, and Joe looked spectacular. Betty glanced down at the cell in her hand. "You know, I don't have your number."

"That's easily remedied." He took the phone, tapped it in, and handed it back.

"Okay, look at the camera." She held up the phone and snapped a picture, attached it to the number, and titled it "Joe." "I like to see who's calling me," she explained, knowing damn well she'd just taken the picture because she wanted to.

"You look…" His gaze scanned her head to toe. "Amazing."

"You don't look too bad yourself." She slipped the phone into her bag and pulled the door behind her.

Joe linked his arm through hers as they walked down the corridor. "I told Charmers I'd come into money," he said. "He warned me off the stock exchange, and said he might have some ideas for me. I'll try to push him again tonight—with Leonora's investment and the recording we should have him, but it would be good to get more to nail him on."

"I wish you'd said that before we left the room," Betty answered. "I have a miniature recording device that looks like a tiepin…" She glanced up at him. "Should we go back and get it?"

Joe's smile was genuine. "You really should consider a change of career. And no, I reckon we'll do fine without it."

They walked into a dining room full of beautifully dressed guests. Double doors to a second room had been opened up for the night, and through it, a casino could be seen. They walked to a cashier's booth set up in the corner of the room, and both changed money into chips. Joe slipped his into his tux pocket, and Betty stowed hers in her bag.

People were making their way to the tables, and the rallymeister stood up and tapped his glass. Joe and Betty took their seats.

"Ladies and gentlemen, this year's Meadowsweet Vintage Rally is almost over. We'll be setting out early tomorrow morning and taking a more direct route to ensure that everyone has plenty of time to get home, get rested, and get ready for the Hunter's Moon Festival tomorrow night." He raised his glass. "I'd like to thank you all for being excellent competitors. We have lost a few cars along the way—unfortunately not every vehicle was robust enough to stay the course—but we will be reunited with our fallen contestants tomorrow at the awards ceremony in Meadowsweet, which will be in the town hall at six, before the Hunter's Moon Festival. Please make sure that you all remember to attend." He waggled his eyebrows. "There will be prizes. And trophies. And the final winners' jerseys."

Two folded jerseys sat next to his place at the table. "And speaking of jerseys"—he looked down at his notes— "we have today's jerseys to present to the team that made the most accurate time today. Could Betty and Joe come up to the stage please?"

Joe took her hand as they stood. She slipped an arm around his waist, and he hugged her close. Her heart tightened. Soon, the operation would be over. The room applauded as they walked up and received their jerseys. "I hope you'll come on the rally next year," the rallymeister said. "It's great to have some younger people along."

Next year. A lifetime away.

# TEN

In her gold wrapping, she was like an expensive gift that he couldn't afford. She moved through the room with a natural ease, automatically accepted by the wealthy rally competitors. *Because she belongs.* Whenever he'd seen her in Meadowsweet, sneaking along after Charmers, this side of Betty had been completely hidden. Even once they'd formally met, at Mark's house and during the practice runs for the rally, she'd dressed casually, just as Alice did. Nothing about her screamed money. But here, she was in her element.

Her clothing and jewelry were obviously expensive. She might not live like someone with money, but privilege was in her genes—in half of her DNA, anyway. When this was over, if he met her mother, what would her reaction be to the idea of her daughter dating an agent? One who'd come so far from the other side of the tracks he was practically shunted into a siding?

*Her father had been a mechanic.*

But they were so different. Her mother cared about her friends knowing that she'd been conned out of some money. His mother had cared about keeping food in their bellies.

"The Corvette didn't make it. Ed Fleming and his wife are heading home in a courtesy car tomorrow. He says he's looking forward to taking it easy in the backseat." Leonora's words broke into his thoughts. She pointed discreetly across the room. "But I don't think he minds being out of the rally one hoot."

The writer, clutching a tiny handheld video camera, was circling the room, filming.

"What's he…" Betty started.

"Apparently it's research," Leonora said. "He told me he takes it everywhere to capture inspiration."

Betty grinned. "I love the idea of the rally being inspiration for a new TV series or something, don't you?"

"You're a real fan of that TV show, aren't

you, Betty? Owning a script must be very exciting."

She nodded. "It's the perfect present."

Charmers caught Joe's eye. A slow smile started on his face, and a calculating glint was in his eye. "Yes, Joe chose well." That look made Joe's hackles rise. It was the sort of look a proud father might give to a son. Or Fagin to one of his pickpocketing boys.

His blood ran cold.

"Ah, here's dinner." Charmers leaned back as a plate was laid before him.

His knowledge of gambling ran to poker, slots, and once or twice, betting on horse races. Betty, on the other hand, was a natural at the tables. They hung around the baccarat table for a while, then she introduced him to roulette.

"Misspent youth," she whispered. "I'm pretty good at poker, too."

"For money, I guess."

"Of course." Her mouth curved in a smile. "Me, Mel, and Alice used to have a Saturday night game—it was fun."

"High rollers, huh?"

"We played for pennies, so not exactly. Although those games could get heated. We don't get to play so much anymore. Alice has

Mark, and now Mel and Heath are getting serious so we don't spend as much time together. I think he's going to propose while they're in the Amazon. Alice thinks so too."

"Will that change things? At the garage, I mean. Heath works away a lot, doesn't he?"

"He can choose to be based anywhere really, and Mel is where he wants to be." She moved on to the craps table, picked up the dice, and brought her hand to his mouth. "Blow on them, for luck."

"I thought only beautiful women blew on dice." But he did as she said, and blew on them anyway.

The dice tumbled on the table, and the others around the table murmured approval as the croupier announced the result and slid a pile of chips her direction.

"It seems to work with beautiful men too."

Joe glanced around the room and spotted Leonora, Charmers, and a stranger seated at a poker table. "Come on." Holding Betty's hand, he walked over.

"We have room for one more. Joe, will you join us?" Charmers asked.

He glanced at Betty, who nodded.

"Texas Hold'em," Charmers advised as Joe

took his seat and placed a stack of chips on the table in front of him. "And I should warn you, I like to win."

Half an hour later, the pile of chips had reduced significantly, and with a smile, Joe counted himself out. Charmers hadn't lied; he played to win, and did—consistently.

"Maybe I should try the slot machines instead." He slipped the chips into his pocket.

Charmers glanced over at Betty. "Being confident enough to lose money is always attractive to a certain type of woman," he said quietly enough that the rest of the table couldn't overhear. "If you're still interested in investing, I may have a proposition for you at the end of the week."

Not soon enough. By then, they'd have him in custody. Joe stood. "I'll look forward to it." With a smile, he walked to Betty.

The day was catching up with him fast. "Let's go sit for a while." Taking two glasses of sparkling champagne from a waiter, Joe led her to a couple of red velvet armchairs on either side of a fireplace on the back wall. It was quiet here, away from the rest of the guests who clustered around the gaming tables.

"Anything?" she asked once they were out of earshot.

"He offered to advise me on investing, but not until the end of the week."

"And you're not exactly James Bond at the tables."

He shook his head. "Gambling's not really my thing. I see a lot of people whose lives have been destroyed by it. It starts innocently enough, ten dollars here and there, and before they know it, they're betting the week's wages and worse. We're a financial crime unit. So gambling, all manner of cons, internet scams, that sort of thing. It all comes down to money."

She crossed her legs, revealing a glimpse of smooth thigh, and nodded. "Money can ruin things. But it can be used for good too. The money raised last night and tonight will help fund a shelter in Meadowsweet—the people here tonight get to have fun and be proud of themselves for helping a really worthy cause."

He knew firsthand what a lifeline a shelter could be for people who needed it, but now wasn't the time to share any more confidences. He'd already opened up to her more than he had to anyone. She swallowed the last mouthful of her champagne and yawned. "Man, I'm tired."

Joe took her glass and deposited it on a nearby table. "Let's go."

They detoured into his room for a moment where he collected some clothes, then continued into her room. "I should retrieve the recording device. I want to hear Charmers ask Leonora to invest."

"Shouldn't we leave it there until after the rally? He might let something else slip."

"You're probably right." He undid the tie that had been strangling him all evening, and took off his tux jacket. Betty stood in the middle of the room. Her gaze was steady and the golden dress glittered.

"Could you"—she gestured over her bare shoulder— "unzip me?"

She didn't turn around—didn't present her back to him. In a couple of steps they were toe to toe. "Did I tell you how much I like this dress?" He smoothed his hands over her soft shoulders, then reached behind her to edge the zipper down a fraction.

Her sigh ignited his senses. She leaned in, and he breathed in the scent of her as his mouth found hers. Tonight was a special night. Their last night together on the rally—before life intruded and took him away from her. He slid the zipper all the way down, and the dress slipped down, pooling at her feet. Beneath it, she wore an ivory garment—maybe it was a teddy?

He pulled back and looked. Strapless and fitted, the lace clung to her curves. A tiny lace bow between her breasts matched bows on the straps that dropped front and back on her thighs.

His mouth dried. "A garter belt?"

Her slow smile lit a fuse that raced through him like wildfire. "Unwrap me."

BETTY SNUGGLED DOWN IN BED. Joe had returned to his own room half an hour earlier, to dress and pack, and she really should be getting up and doing the same. Another five minutes. She pulled up the duvet around her ears, reached for Joe's pillow, wrapped her arms around it, and pressed her face into the cool cotton. His scent lingered. Last night had been more than sex; she'd been making love, and he had too—it was apparent in every touch, in the look in the depths of his eyes, in the sure and steady way he brought her to heaven in a heartbeat.

At one point, she'd almost told him exactly how important he was to her, exactly how much she wanted to be with him, not just for a day or a week, but caution had stilled the words in her throat. She'd known the clock was ticking on their relationship, but now that the time to part was almost here, she wasn't ready—wasn't prepared for the moment of his departure.

Almost an hour later, she was drying her hair when there was a rap at the door.

She opened it with a smile and looked at Joe's chest. "Oh, that's a good idea. Hang on, I'll change." She stripped off her sky-blue cotton shirt and changed it for the emerald-green winners' jersey they'd earned the day before. "What do you think?"

"I prefer you without it." His voice was husky. "But I guess we better go grab some breakfast." He pulled her close and kissed her.

"I'm not really that hungry."

He shook his head. "Don't tempt me. We have about forty-five minutes before they hand out the route books, and a ton of things to do before then." He nipped at her earlobe. "We just don't have enough time." He stepped away and took her hand. "Come on."

She followed him into the dining room. "Bacon and eggs?" Joe waved the waitress over.

"Of course."

He cast a look over her body. "I swear, I don't know where you put it. There's not an ounce of fat on you."

The waitress stood next to their table, so pushing away thoughts of their naked bodies, she ordered for both of them.

Knowledge that it was the last day of the rally bound the competitors together, simmered in the air as the navigators plotted the route onto the last day's maps. Joe and some of the other drivers were talking and laughing—he'd fitted in easily to the group, and had even been approached about some of his furniture that was for sale in the furniture shop in town. If his business were real, he'd have made some valuable contacts this trip.

"Five minutes," the rallymeister said.

Betty stroked the final few instructions onto the map with her highlighter, gathered up her paperwork, and straightened.

"Good luck." Leonora was doing the same on the other side of the large table. She had put all her things into a bag, except for a ballpoint pen with a button on top that she absentmindedly clicked on and off with her thumb. She looked fresh and free this morning, no doubt relieved that this entire operation was almost at an end.

"You too. Not long now." They shared a private smile, then separated to find their drivers.

Moments later, with their time recorded, Joe started the engine. "I'm going to miss this car." He ran a hand over the top of the steering wheel. "Maybe I'll search out one of these myself. I love driving it."

"There's a place in Chesapeake that could source one for you. Under the Hood could maintain it for you." She was talking as though he was going to be around, as though he wasn't racing back to his life in Chicago within days. She looked down at the route book and swallowed. "I guess you could probably find one in Chicago too."

He rested a hand on her thigh. "Sometime next month we'll take a trip out to Chesapeake together, and check that place out."

"Next month?"

Joe smiled. "Yeah, I reckon I'm due some vacation time."

Betty's heart rate quickened. Did he mean he'd be back for a week or two and hoped to have a quick fling, or did he mean more—that they might...

Betty blinked away all thought of their uncertain future and concentrated. "This route is going to be easy. We're taking the quick way back. Take a right in half a mile, then go straight for ten."

Joe returned his hand to the steering wheel and released the hand brake. "Okay."

The day was clear and bright. Sunlight bleeding through the canopy above dappled the ground ahead. It had been too long since she'd taken time out—had escaped from the pressure of work to just enjoy the scenery. Had pressed the reset switch on her life.

"Right here." She ticked the instruction off the route map. "Ten miles straight on. Charmers is going to run when Josh De Witt appears, isn't he?"

"Probably, but we're ready for him. Bond and the team are already set up in the Meadowsweet Grand." Joe switched gears. "Charmers might play nice for a while. Cutting and running is likely to arouse suspicion, but I imagine he'll transfer the money from his account to his *real* account immediately. We're watching both accounts, and the moment he does the transfer we've got him."

Her heart dipped. *And that would be the end of it.* "Is there anything I can do?"

"You've done enough already. I wished you and Leonora weren't involved, but without both of you we wouldn't be where we are today." His mouth curved in a smile. "What happens at the end of the race?"

"Once all the competitors have passed the finish line, we only have about an hour and a half before the presentation ceremony. Apparently they want to get it over with before people join their families and get ready for the Hunter's Moon Festival. Leonora said she and Charmers are heading home quickly so she can transfer the money into his account. He told her the investment is time-sensitive and he needs to do the transfer before close of business today."

"We need that recording device."

Betty nodded. "I know. All the cars will be parked outside the town hall. She knows the recording device is only stuck up under the dash with tape so she's going to retrieve it and slip it to me before they take a taxi home."

"Great. I'll distract him while you two handle that. Then I'll drop it off to Bond at the hotel and meet you back for the presentation ceremony."

Excitement danced in Betty's chest. They had everything covered. The team was in place, and even if Charmers tried to run, there was no way this could go wrong now. She wished she could join Joe with his team at the hotel, that they could see this whole affair out together— but explaining her presence would no doubt be impossible.

"Wouldn't it be neat if we won?" She checked the stopwatch against the route book. "Our time is good, but we're slightly ahead— slow it down a little."

# ELEVEN

It was late afternoon as they coasted across the finish line in Meadowsweet. The crowds were out along the route to welcome them home, just as they had been on the way out.

Three days, hardly long enough for the seismic shift that had happened since they were last in town.

Charmers's capture was within reach. And after it was done, there would be others. More strangers to track across the country, to bring to justice. The thought held little appeal. Maybe he'd been undercover too long—focused on the bad stuff people did to each other. All that awaited him back in Chicago was a place he existed in, not somewhere he actually lived.

When he'd first driven into Meadowsweet weeks ago, it had just been another place. Another stop on the route. Now, the people and the town itself had pulled him in, accepted him. He had one good friend here, and the possibility of making a lot more, if they could accept his deceiving them for so long.

And Betty. He stopped at the time control point, and Betty handed their card out of the window for the time to be recorded. She whooped, and waved it at him. "Perfect time! No penalties!" Her eyes shone.

He cupped her radiant face in his hands and kissed her.

"Okay, we should drive down to town hall," Betty said. She rolled down the window and looked back up the road. "Here they come."

BOND and five other FBI agents had taken over a room in the Meadowsweet Grand Hotel. Two computers were set up in the living area, and the side table was stacked with paperwork.

Bond ushered Joe in. "Okay, here's what's going to happen."

Bond walked around the room as he spoke. "Murphy will stay here listening to the tape."

"Hey, Joe," Patrick Murphy said. "Good to see you."

Joe'd worked with this team on more cases than he cared to count. They were all good men, good agents. A tight-knit group he'd never taken the time to really get to know. Work had always come first. For the first time, the years at the bureau seemed sterile and empty.

"You too, Patrick."

Bond walked up behind the two agents at computers. "Jackson and DeSilva are watching the accounts. The minute money starts moving, we'll see it."

Another agent, Rory Johnson, walked over. "Someone is here to see you, Joe."

Joe met Mark at the door.

"I brought the recording device." Mark held it out. "I guess you're busy, so…"

"Thanks," Joe said. "I'm sorry I couldn't tell you about all this—I wanted to. I normally don't get close to people when I'm undercover, but this trip—" He shook his head. It was crazy to think he had a chance of keeping a friendship based on half truths alive. They'd spent long lazy afternoons doing guy stuff together. Fishing in the stream that ran down the back of the property. Talking about women and cracking beers. The companionship had grown until Mark was like the brother he'd never had. Losing him sucked.

"I reckon you only lied about the details." Mark stared him in the eye. "You're still the same guy underneath."

"Yeah. Only what I had to, and now that the secret's out, you know everything."

"And Betty—she seems to be pretty into you. Was caring about her an act too?"

Joe's back stiffened. For a second he wanted to tell Mark to mind his own business. Then he took a long, hard look at his friend. *Her* friend. Remembered the sort of man Mark was.

"It started that way, for both of us. We had to pretend to be a couple because Charmers saw us together…" He ran a hand through his hair. "He would have caught her following him—I had to intervene, and, well, I kissed her. I had no intention of going any further but…"

"I care about those women. All three of them." Mark's eyebrows pulled together as he frowned.

"I care about Betty." *More than care.* "When this is all over I want to be with her. I'm winging it here, but I have to make it work. Life without her would be damned boring."

Johnson loped over. "Bond wants to talk."

"I'll go." Mark thumped Joe on the arm and glanced into the room. "You look like you have backup covered, but remember, I've got your back too." He walked away down the corridor. Joe closed the door and returned to his boss.

Bond was at DeSilva's desk, staring intently at the screen.

"Something?" Joe asked.

"Leonora De Witt just made the transfer into Charmers's account." Bond straightened. "With luck he'll move it into the Carlisle account before the presentation ceremony."

Joe checked his watch. "We only have about three-quarters of an hour." He glanced around the suite, noting the remains of room service on a tray near the door. *I need coffee.*

"Here's the recording device." He hooked it up and sat down to listen. The conversation was very much as it had been in the MG, with Leonora giving navigation directions. The recording was clear and distinct. Leonora said, "Do you want a drink?"

Charmers answered, "Yes," Then a noise

was heard as though she were unfastening a cooler to retrieve a drink.

"This could take a while. There's hours of recording to review." He rubbed a hand over the ache at the curve of his spine. "I might call out for coffee…"

"Sure," Bond said. "Call room service."

While waiting for the coffee, Joe contacted Betty and arranged to meet her outside the town hall. By the time the coffee had been ordered, delivered, and drunk it was almost time to leave.

Bond called one of the agents over. "Murphy, you know what we're listening for. Stay here and monitor this." He clapped his hands. "Everyone get set, we're going to stake out the town hall. When Josh De Witt makes his appearance we might expect Charmers to make a break for it."

Murphy nodded.

"Sir." Jackson stood up and turned from the computer.

"We got it. Charmers has just shunted the money into the Carlisle account."

SHE WAS WAITING outside the town hall. Dressed in black jeans that molded over her curves and a V-neck sweater in that funny color somewhere between blue and green. She stepped from foot to foot, looked up the road and back, waiting for someone. Waiting for him. The exact moment she saw him she stilled and smiled.

He walked over and kissed her, feeling the soft wool of her sweater under his hands as he pulled her close.

"Leonora and Charmers arrived a minute ago," she said. "They're inside."

Everyone was crowded into a barely-big-enough room in the town hall. The rallymeister stood at a table at the back of the room, but there wasn't enough seating, so the majority stood. Joe located Charmers and Leonora at the back and stood next to them.

"I'm not going to keep you very long," the rallymeister said. "I know you all want to get back to your families and ready for the Hunter's Moon Festival."

He lied.

It took three-quarters of an hour to hand out prizes and thank everyone involved. Representatives from the hotel and places they'd stopped for lunch were thanked, and the team responsible for time control was congratulated for doing such a good job. Charmers smiled. "These things take forever, don't they?"

Before Joe could answer, the rallymeister spoke again.

"And now, the final prize. The winners' cup. I'm delighted to say that the winners of this year's rally are…" He waited a few seconds, like those annoying people on TV talent shows. "Joe and Betty! Come on up, guys!"

Betty was gripping his hand so tight it had gone numb. Her wide grin forced an answering one from him as she dragged him up onto the stage to accept the silver cup. Everyone clapped, genuinely happy for them.

This was home. This was where he was supposed to be, with this woman at his side. Joe snaked an arm around Betty's waist as they returned to the back of the room—back to Charmers and Leonora.

"I have one final announcement to make," the rallymeister looked around the room until he found Leonora. "Leonora, can you come up to the stage please?"

She looked puzzled, but walked up the aisle between the seats to the front anyway.

Charmers turned to Joe. "Do you know what this is about?"

Joe shook his head.

"We have a very special guest this evening. Someone who's come a long way to be here with us, someone who is part of our community, that I know you'll all be very happy to welcome home. Ladies and gentlemen, all the way from Afghanistan, Josh De Witt!"

Leonora gasped as a door at the back of the room opened and her son walked through. The room burst into applause as she ran to her son and threw her arms around him.

Joe turned to Charmers.

The older man pulled a handkerchief from the top pocket of his tweed jacket and dabbed his forehead. His gaze flickered to the door. Joe took a step closer. "Are you all right?"

"I'm not feeling too well," Charmers murmured. "The heat in here…I think, I think I need some fresh air." He glanced at the door again.

"I'll help you." Joe grasped his arm.

"I…yes, thank you." Charmers undid the top button of his shirt, slid a finger around the inside of his collar and started to move. Everyone's attention was on Leonora and Josh as

Josh started to speak—to thank them for the welcome and explain how he'd managed to return home early to surprise his mother. There was no time to talk to Betty, who'd moved back so Charmers could pass.

The hunter's moon shone down, bathing the scene in light as they walked from the town hall. "Do go back inside," Charmers urged. "I'll be fine. I'll join you in a moment."

Four dark-clad figures approached from all sides.

Charmers's eyes widened. "What…"

Joe stared into his quarry's eyes and spoke the words he'd waited a lifetime to say. "I'm FBI, Alexander. You're under arrest."

---

BETTY WALKED toward the park in the center of town with Alice and Mark. It was strange to be at the Hunter's Moon Festival without Joe. Large barbecues were set up, and the park was set out with tables and chairs. A stage had been erected—local bands would take turns entertaining the audience, which ranged from young to old. A fairground was set up, surrounded by a number of stalls. One selling cotton candy, others with games. There was even a small striped tent with a large sign outside stating Madam Mystery—fortune teller.

The arrest outside the town hall was all anyone wanted to talk about. Some recounted how they'd seen Charmers taken away to the police station in handcuffs. Some how they'd seen him bundled into a black van and driven away. Everyone was concerned for Leonora— until she revealed that she hadn't been taken in, that she'd been instrumental in bringing him to justice.

Ed Fleming was annoyed he'd managed to miss filming the moment. Cassie White, the *Meadowsweet Echo's* only reporter, was on a desperate hunt for details for the next morning's paper.

The huge blood-red moon made the night strange and magical, shone through the night, casting an unreal light over the spectacle. Betty's cell phone rang, interrupting her reverie.

"We got him," Joe said. "I'm going to be tied up here doing paperwork…and then there'll be a debriefing… I don't know when I can get away."

"I'm at the festival but I don't know how long I'll stay. I'm exhausted. Call me when you can, okay?" Betty slipped her cell into her pocket and linked hands with her friends.

It was over. Finally over. The man she'd pursued, the man who had stolen from her mother, was finally in custody.

So where was the feeling of elation?

# TWELVE

The arrest and debriefing continued for hours. When it was finally over, Bond handed Joe a hotel room key.

"Get some sleep," he said. "You did well, Joe."

Too keyed up to sleep, he decided to take a long, hot shower to ease his aching muscles. For so long he'd been focused on the moment of Charmers's capture. Adrenaline had coursed through his veins, keeping his body in a state of urgent readiness. Now, in drama's aftermath, exhaustion made his limbs heavy but his mind still raced. If it weren't so late he'd call Betty— talk through the events of the evening, celebrate with her.

He climbed out of the shower. Yawned as he wrapped a towel around his waist. Who was he kidding—he no longer had the energy to stumble to the bed; celebrating was totally out of the question.

If she were here, he'd curl up with her in bed. Wrap his arms around her. Maybe talk quietly about the capture. But mostly, just enjoy having her by his side. His stomach growled, but he was too tired to even think of ordering anything from room service.

There was a knock at the door.

He tightened the towel around his waist and opened it.

Bond stalked in, eyes blazing. "Did you know?" Fury rolled off him in waves. "Did you know what that stupid girlfriend of yours was doing?"

Disconcerted by his boss's presence and attitude, Joe just stood there. Confusion clouded his mind. "What are you talking about?"

"Betty Smith." Bond closed the door. "Did you know that she put the investment money into Leonora's account one day before Leonora paid it out?"

"No."

"Yes." Bond glared at Joe. "We had him

cold, but now…I don't have to tell you, but it looks bad. The daughter of a woman Charmers previously conned funded this takedown."

Bond must have got it wrong. "She couldn't have. There must be some mistake."

"Get dressed and come next door." Bond's jaw flexed. "I'll play you the tape."

Once Bond had left, Joe dressed quickly and walked back into the FBI's suite. Bond must have gotten it wrong. In the long days in the MG they'd talked ceaselessly about what Betty and Leonora had tagged "Operation Charmers." Betty hadn't given any hint that she was the one putting up the money. His stomach churned as he walked to Murphy. The burly agent handed over headphones without a word. His somber face told a story Joe didn't want to hear.

When Joe nodded, he started the recording, and a conversation bled through the headphones.

"How much?" Betty's familiar voice.

"Twenty thousand. Are you sure you want to risk it?

Twenty thousand is a lot of money. If this all goes wrong…" Leonora replied.

Joe held his breath, hoping, praying that

somehow Murphy and Bond had gotten it wrong, that she hadn't really...

"It won't. And I have the funds and your account details. I'll transfer it to your account tonight." Betty's familiar voice was a hammer smashing his hopes to smithereens.

---

BETTY HAD SLIPPED AWAY from the celebrations around midnight. Had walked straight inside, climbed the stairs, stripped, and crawled into bed. There'd been no further word from Joe, but that wasn't surprising. There'd be time enough tomorrow.

Moonlight bled in from the gap between the drapes, so she turned over and closed her eyes. There was something wonderful about being home in her own bed. To have her own pillow under her head, and the familiar weight of her duvet covering her exhausted body. The only thing that could be better, that would make it perfect, was if Joe were here by her side.

The insistent, repeated peal of the doorbell woke her from a deep, dreamless sleep. "I'm coming, I'm coming," she muttered as the doorbell continued to ring. She pulled on her robe and staggered downstairs to the front door.

She turned on the outside light and peered through the peephole.

*Joe.* Eager anticipation made her fingers fumble as she undid the chain. With the news of Charmers's capture she'd longed to see him—to celebrate their success. Going to the Hunter's Moon Festival with Alice, Mark, and the others had been fun, but unsatisfying due to his absence. She brushed her hair back with her fingers. Then with a smile, unlocked the door and opened it. "What time is..." Her words trailed off at one look at his face.

There were dark shadows under his eyes. His mouth was pressed together in a tight line. His hands hung at his sides; he made no move to embrace her—just stepped inside. No joy, no jubilation. Instead, he looked tired, disillusioned, beaten.

"I just want to know one thing. I want to know why." He pushed a hand through hair so mussed it was as if he'd being doing that all night. His eyebrows were pulled together, creases forming parallel lines between them. "I thought I knew you. I just don't understand."

Still he made no move to touch her. She took

a step forward, and he took one back, as though she were the bearer of some contagion. Her sleep-muddled brain couldn't make sense of his words, of his attitude.

"What's wrong?"

"You know damn well what's wrong." He rubbed a hand over the back of his neck. The expression on his face morphed from resignation to anger. "I didn't want to believe it. I told my boss he must have made a mistake, that I knew you, that we were honest with each other. But then I heard your voice…"

Panic flared as realization dawned. *That day in the car… Leonora…* "Joe, I…" How could she explain? "She didn't have the money readily available, it was the only way to catch him, I…"

His expression hardened. "When did you make this decision?"

She had to make him understand, had to fix this. Betty breathed in deep, and gripped the lapels of her robe. "Long before I met you. Leonora and I talked it out at the very beginning. It was always our understanding that I would provide the money to bait Charmers—I had to do something."

His shoulders slumped. He looked away. "So you've known. All this time. This wasn't a spurof-the-moment decision. At any time during the trip you could have opened up and told me about it." He shook his head in disbelief. "I told you everything. That I was responsible for him getting away the last time. I even told you about my mother." He stepped toward the door.

*No!* This couldn't be happening—after all they'd been through together, after catching Charmers, one little mistake couldn't tear them apart. "Joe…" She reached for him.

"No." He jerked away. His eyes blazed. "You didn't trust me, did you? Couldn't give away control for a second."

Betty crossed her arms. "I did. I do. I wanted to get him as much as you did, and he's in custody, isn't he? It worked." She wasn't going to apologize for what she'd done; Leonora didn't have the money, and she did. Everything she'd done to catch him was logical. But deep inside a suspicion lurked that maybe he was right—maybe she hadn't been able to trust him enough to tell him everything.

"The daughter of one of Charmers's previous victims gave bait money to another woman he was going to con. While working with the embittered undercover FBI agent with a score to settle."

"But you didn't—"

"It doesn't matter that I didn't know. Charmers's defense will have a field day with it. It looks like entrapment—shifts from him scamming Leonora to a deliberate, premeditated attempt by us to entrap him. The legal team are on it, but this could be enough to totally destroy the case." He reached for the door handle.

Panic fluttered inside like a bird desperate for escape. She couldn't lose him now, had to make him understand, make him forgive her. "I made a mistake. I wanted to catch him, I didn't think…"

"No, you didn't." Condemnation flattened his tone. "You didn't think, and you didn't trust. If at any stage you'd trusted me enough to come clean, we could have discussed it, could have ensured this didn't happen. I can't be with someone who doesn't trust me."

Her heart cracked into two at his words, at the look in his eyes.

He jerked the door open, walked down the path, and didn't look back.

# THIRTEEN

Betty couldn't do anything to turn back time. Couldn't press rewind back to the beginning of their relationship and do over. But she could and would do something.

So she'd packed a bag, organized her trip, and at eleven the following morning picked up the phone and dialed her mother's number.

"I'm flying out to see you today, Mom. I've booked my flight," she said when her mother answered. "I'm sorry for the short notice, but we need to talk, and it's urgent."

"I know," Christine said, her voice so calm Betty's shattered nerves quieted. "I was letting you sleep in this morning before I called you. Joe telephoned early and explained that they had seventy-two hours to hold Charmers before they had to charge him. Helen and I have just given our statements to a very charming FBI agent."

Stunned, Betty sank down onto the nearest chair. "You spoke to Joe?" He'd known she wanted to see her mother, talk to her face-to-face —but he'd gone ahead and contacted her, arranged this… Her chest hurt, as though a steel bolt had been pushed through her heart.

"He explained that time was of the essence, darling. I wish you'd phoned me first before booking the flight." Her voice was warm and comforting. "Although if you can manage to get a few days away, I'd love to see you. Can you still make it?"

Mel and Heath were back this weekend, and the thought of being with her friends, accepting their sympathy for the end of her relationship, made her shudder inside. Her heart felt raw— she didn't think she could stand to face anyone.

She'd call from the airport—Alice would understand.

"Yes, Mom. I'm coming anyway. I'll call you as the train nears Westhampton. Can you pick me up at the station?"

TWELVE HOURS LATER, she walked out of Westhampton train station—bag in hand—and found her mother waiting.

"You look so tired, darling." Christine drove her quickly home. She unlocked the front door, turned on the light, and walked into the kitchen. "I'll make some tea. The rally just finished yesterday, you should have taken some time to recuperate."

"I couldn't." For all the long hours traveling, she'd kept an iron grip on her emotions, but now the iron melted. "I've screwed up, Mom. I think I've ruined everything."

Over tea she told her mother everything. Even about Joe.

When she had no more words, Christine spoke. "You know I love you, darling. But you've got to stop trying to wrap me in cotton wool. I'm in my fifties, not my seventies. Alexander wasn't my first lover after your father, and he won't be my last."

Betty blinked.

Christine gave a wry smile. "I know you don't want to think of me having relationships, but I have. And I do. I'm a woman, not a saint." They were sitting close on one of the large white sofas in the sitting room. Christine reached over and grasped Betty's hand. "You've always been protective—I appreciate that, and your father would, too, if he were here. You've looked out for me, and I guess I've let you."

Her mouth tightened. "After talking to Joe the other day, I called Helen Dawkins and apologized. I took the easy option by not reporting Alexander. I should have stepped up. When Joe called this morning I told him right away to send an agent out to take our statements."

Betty shook her head. "You…"

"Secrets destroy lives. I'm not going to stay silent anymore. I told the FBI every single detail of my time with Alexander. Helen and I will testify against him and make sure he goes away for good."

Betty blinked back tears. Her heart filled with love and admiration for the woman her mother was, the woman who'd bravely made the decision to bare the truth of being deceived publicly.

"There's just one more thing," Christine said. "You have to let go of the feeling that you bore any responsibility by not coming to meet Alexander. Yes, I was taken in, but so was Helen, and her daughter lives five minutes away and even met him. He's a professional con artist. I don't blame myself for being taken in by him— anyone would be."

"That's what Joe said."

"Joe sounds like a very insightful man." Christine smiled.

THEY'D HAD seventy-two hours to hold Charmers without charge and to Joe's relief, hadn't needed all of them. The sworn testimonies of Christine Tremaine and Helen Dawkins were enough to bring formal charges against him and schedule a trial.

He should have been ecstatic.

The errors of the past were behind him. Life went on. But there was no joy in it. Every day was the same. He got up, dressed, and went to the office. The world had faded to gray, empty and unremarkable now that the goal that had obsessed him for so long was over. On Friday, a group of guys from work headed out to the bar for their regular drinking session. When he'd asked to join them, the response had hammered home how isolated he'd become.

They'd said yes, but had mentioned that he'd never joined them before.

Four years. And every night he'd been so caught up in work, he'd never even tried to socialize. His narrow life had expanded out in Meadowsweet and contracted back on returning to Chicago. He missed his workshop, the ability to lose himself in anything creative. The traffic, the noise, the continual bitter taste in the air, painted his mood black.

"Can I see you for a minute, Joe?" Bond asked.

He pushed back his chair and followed Bond into his office, closing the door behind him.

Bond pushed a manila folder across the desk to him. "This expenses chit came in for bidding at the charity auction during the Charmers case. A script for *Crime Bites*. I need you to sign off on canceling it."

She'd been so excited… "I'd like to take it over instead, if that's okay."

Bond frowned, flicked the folder open, and checked the document inside. "Are you sure? It's a lot of money."

Joe nodded. The bid had not only been for charity, it had been the perfect gift. For Betty, anyway.

"Okay, fine. I'll clear that with the financial department." He leaned back in his swivel chair. "Other business. Jackson has been working an internet scam—one of the 'help me get my millions out of a bank' ones. He's made contact and is ready to take it to the next phase. I thought you could go in undercover."

Another job. Another town. The general feeling of dissatisfaction expanded out into full-blown revolt at the idea of embedding himself in another community for months on end. "I don't think I can do it."

Bond's eyes widened. "Are you saying you don't want to work in the field any longer?"

The other option was a desk job, based full-time in the office. The FBI had been his life for years now, but what did he have to show for it apart from a regular wage? Joe ran his hand through his hair. *Could I have a different life?* The furniture business in Meadowsweet had been a cover, but there was a genuine demand for his pieces. The cabin had been perfect—and he'd signed a six-month lease. And Meadowsweet had Betty. Betty. He'd shoved her out of his waking reality, but couldn't banish her from his dreams. Despite the fact that she hadn't trusted him enough to know that he wouldn't screw up if she shared everything with him, a part of him couldn't let go, couldn't say goodbye. She'd called, and texted, but rather than have that final conversation, drive a nail through the coffin of their relationship once and for all, he'd ignored all of her attempts to contact him.

When he'd confessed that he was the agent who'd let Charmers walk the first time, she'd managed to get past it—had managed to forgive. He couldn't make sense of his churning emotions when it came to Betty, but he couldn't definitively end it either. Being miles away brooding wasn't working; it was time to face the problem head-on.

"I'm burned out." The words came from the heart. "I think my time here is through."

"You want to transfer…"

Joe shook his head. "I'm handing in my notice. I'll work out the month, but then I'm leaving the FBI for good."

# FOURTEEN

Mel walked into the conference room where the three owners of Under the Hood were holding their morning meeting—which had always been, and continued to be, an excuse to drink coffee and eat pastries before starting work for the day.

She put a thick manila envelope in front of Betty. "This just came in the mail."

Betty ripped it open and pulled out the *Crime Bites* script Joe had bid on. "This can't be right—the FBI…" Her words trailed into silence as a piece of paper fluttered out.

*I want you to have this.*

The letter *J* was scrawled underneath.

Betty's chest ached as though it had been crushed in a vise. Tears blurred her vision.

"What is it?" Mel asked.

Wordlessly she handed the note over. Mel read it and passed it to Alice.

"You know what this means, don't you?" Alice said. "It means he forgives you."

"He hasn't taken any of my calls, or responded to my texts." On returning to Meadowsweet she'd been buoyed with hope that the fact that Charmers had been charged for conning Christine and Helen would be enough.

That he might forgive her, and they might have another chance. So she'd called him and left messages. None of which he'd answered. She'd texted, too, but his silence was as eloquent as any response could have been.

He didn't want to talk. Wasn't prepared to listen to any heartfelt apologies. Didn't want her any more. She'd tried to stop talking about the pain in her shredded heart. Had tried not to be envious when Mel and Heath had announced that she'd accepted his proposal on their last night in the Amazon, and that they were going to be married.

Had tried without success to stop crying herself to sleep every night.

"Mark heard from him last week. This is his last week with the FBI," Alice whispered.

Shock stabbed through Betty. "Were you even going to tell me?"

Alice glanced away. "Mark didn't tell me the details and I didn't want to make things worse. I know he hasn't called, and you've been so sad lately—"

They might be over because of something she'd done, but Joe shouldn't lose his job because of it. Betty jumped up. "I'm sorry, guys, but I need to book a flight to Chicago."

---

A PAPERWORK MOUNTAIN was no substitute for the real thing. The air in Joe's tiny office was stale and the view from the window… well, you could hardly call it a view. He puffed out a frustrated breath. Two more weeks, then he'd be back in Meadowsweet. Back to the dusky-blue mountains and his cabin. There was too much between Betty and him to be solved by a phone call or a quick text, but when he was back maybe they could meet and talk it out.

Anything had to be better than life without her.

Patrick Murphy stuck his meaty head around Joe's door. "You might want to go into Bond's office." Going into Bond's office was a routine he was getting darned sick of. His boss was determined to get him to retract his resignation and gave talking-him-out-of-it a shot every day.

"I don't suppose you could just tell him I'm busy?" He waved at the teetering pile of paperwork.

Patrick shook his head. "I'm telling you, Joe, you want to be there." He grinned.

Joe frowned, stood up, and walked around his desk.

There was a buzz in the air. Agents seemed to have stopped working and taken to staring at him instead as he strode to Bond's open office door.

What he saw made him realize why.

Betty.

Dressed in a smart gray skirt and matching jacket with a hot-pink shirt beneath. Nude hose and high heels. Chestnut hair twisted up in a topknot. She stood in front of Bond's desk with her back ramrod straight.

The breath left his lungs at the sight. *God, I've missed her.*

"Come on in, Joe." Bond looked up at his approach, and waved him in. "You need to hear this."

Her gaze darted to him and a nervous smile trembled on her lips. "Hello, Joe."

She looked thinner, as though like him, she couldn't be bothered with food anymore. Pale. "Hi, Betty."

"Miss Smith wishes to make a statement." Bond steepled his fingers.

Joe frowned. A statement? The incongruity of the situation almost made him laugh aloud. *Too many cop shows.* But she wasn't just "in the neighborhood." She'd traveled all the way out there; what on earth could she be there for? "A statement?" he echoed.

"Yes." Bond waved to a chair. "Won't you sit, Miss Smith?"

She shook her head. "I'd prefer not to."

"Betty..." He took a step forward.

"No, Joe. I have to do this." Focusing her gaze on Bond, she twisted her hands together. "I have discovered that this is Joe's last week." She cleared her throat. "I know you must be disappointed, Agent Bond, by the fact that the operation against Charmers was compromised, but I want you to reconsider your decision to fire Joe for it. I made the mistake—Joe didn't know until after the capture that I had transferred money into Leonora's account. He's blameless in this, and a damn good agent."

Her eyes flashed fire and she leaned forward and placed the tips of her fingers on Bond's desk. "We need people like him in the FBI. I'll do anything to get you to reverse this decision. I'll give a statement, I'll take full responsibility in front of a judge, I'll even talk to the press. He's the most trustworthy man I know. He's hardworking, dedicated, and honest. Please give him another chance."

Joe's pulse was racing. She'd do all that for him?

Bond smiled. His gaze moved from Betty's impassioned face to Joe's. "Do you want to tell her or shall I?"

Joe stepped up and took her hand. Stared into her gorgeous face. He could tell her, but first…

He cupped her face and kissed her hard.

Her lips were as soft and yielding as he remembered. He breathed in her familiar scent, loving the feel of her face against his palms. Sounds came from the room behind him—every single agent had heard her words, and their claps and hoots of approval filled in the air. When he finally let her go they were both breathing rapidly.

There was hope in the depths of her eyes. Confusion, as though she didn't understand how her words, her heartfelt declaration, had earned such a reaction.

He let her in on the secret. "I resigned."

"You resigned?" With a gasp, she covered her flushing face with her hands.

"Yeah. I'm leaving." He pulled her hands down and held on to them. "And moving to Meadowsweet."

---

JOE GRABBED her hand and took her into a tiny office. There was nowhere to sit except for the swivel chair behind the desk stacked high with paper. He closed the door firmly. "I'm sorry about that lot." He waved at the closed door. "What can I say, the sight of a pretty woman getting kissed fires them up."

It was so good to see his smile. The smile she'd just about given up on ever seeing again. She reached out and touched the dimple creasing his cheek. Placed the flat of her palm against his skin. "I've missed you."

"I didn't want to call you. When we almost lost the case, I was angry."

"I know." The case was everything. Had always been everything to him, and she'd jeopardized that.

"I was angry that you didn't share the information with me. Which is pretty ironic seeing as I rarely share anything with anyone." His mouth twisted in a wry smile. "I grew up hiding everything. Being self-sufficient. I thought you'd hate me when you found out about the mistake I made years ago with Charmers." He stroked a hand down her arm. "But you didn't. You sucked it up, processed it, and forgave me. I'm sorry that I couldn't forgive you so easily."

"He almost escaped."

Joe nodded. "And when the case looked in danger of falling apart, I realized I didn't care about it half as much as I cared about losing you." He snaked an arm around her waist and pulled her close. "I didn't call you because I didn't want to tell you good-bye. I couldn't walk away while there might be some chance of repairing our relationship."

Betty laid her head against his chest. Felt his heartbeat, strong and true. He'd always been good at repairs. "So you're going to be a carpenter?"

"I'm going to repair things that are broken. Build things. Be with you, if you'll have me. I'm almost finished up here, and then I'll be packing my bags and returning to Meadowsweet."

Betty tilted her head up to his. "I'll be waiting."

# FIFTEEN

## SIX MONTHS LATER...

The bride wore white. She walked out of the tiny Meadowsweet church into the spring sunshine on the arm of her new husband, followed by her two best friends dressed in matching rose-pink bridesmaids' dresses.

Bells pealed out, filling the churchyard with sound. Mel and Heath were swarmed with delighted guests, offering congratulations and snapping pictures.

Alice and Betty stood to one side, watching their friend live her happy ever after. They each had their own best man—it had been too difficult to choose just one, so the groom had broken with tradition to nominate two.

"Ouch." Alice rubbed her stomach.

"Are you okay?" Betty asked.

"He's kicking." Alice winced. "I think he likes the music."

Betty's heart melted as Mark's arm snaked around his very pregnant partner.

"Maybe our son would like another trip up the aisle before he makes an appearance," Mark clutched Alice's hand. "I know you wanted to wait until after he was born, but we have a couple of months and you look so gorgeous in that dress—you'd look even better in a wedding dress."

"I'd look like a giant meringue. I doubt we can organize it that quick..."

"Ah, that's where you're wrong. I've already organized a license and spoken to the priest."

Alice smiled and gave in. "Well, in that case..."

Someone started throwing confetti, and within minutes the sky was filled with pastel petals, as though someone had shaken a cherry tree until it spilled its blossoms.

Betty brushed away a stray heart-shaped fragment of paper from Joe's shoulder. "They look so happy, don't they?" She gazed at Mel and Heath, posing for the wedding photographer. "And they'll love the seat." He'd worked so hard on the beautiful hanging bench for two, carving details of vines and flowers around their friends' entwined names. They'd sneaked out of the wedding rehearsal and installed it on the porch the night before. Heath had stayed the night at their house and Mel at Alice and Mark's, so the newlyweds had yet to see their very special present.

"Do you miss it? The FBI?" He seemed so happy, so content, but sometimes she worried that he'd regret swapping the excitement of investigation for a simple, small-town life.

"I wouldn't trade what we have for anything," Joe said. "And if I feel the need to investigate, I can always raid your stash of fingerprinting powder, bugging devices, and Tyvek suits. Being here, seeing Mel and Heath so happy, makes me impatient for our wedding day."

He ran his thumb over the sapphire-and-gold band on Betty's finger. It would be a few months yet—they'd decided there was only one day they wanted to marry. One moon overhead, the first night they would spend as man and wife.

The hunter's moon.

Betty's mouth parted a fraction as she gazed into his eyes. "You know what?"

"What?" He pulled her close.

Betty smiled. "I love a happy ending."

Printed in Great Britain
by Amazon

64939931R00135